ANOTHER
FORM OF
DARKNESS

Edited by
*Paula Dias Garcia
Sam Agar,
Marc Clohessy
& Issy Flower*

**LIMERICK
2023**

ANOTHER NAME FOR DARKNESS
ISBN: 978 1 7391383 5 6
PUBLISHED BY Sans. PRESS
December 2023
Limerick, Republic of Ireland

COVER ARTWORK & ILLUSTRATIONS by WOLFSKULLJACK
LAYOUT & BOOK DESIGN by Paula Dias Garcia
TYPESET in Warnock Pro and Benguiat Pro ITC

EDITORS
Paula Dias Garcia, Sam Agar, Marc Clohessy & Issy Flower

www.sanspress.com
@PressSans
sans.press
/sans.press

ANOTHER NAME FOR DARKNESS receives
financial assistance from the Arts Council.

EDITOR'S NOTE

Paula Dias Garcia

Considering the inspirations that helped build *Another Name for Darkness* – from the visual imagery to the quotes chosen for our submission call – it was hardly a surprise for our team when many of the stories pointed out how often darkness was hiding inside, both in ourselves and those very close to us. Sometimes malicious, sometimes borne out of neglect, the darkness in these stories didn't come crashing through in the night; rather, it seemed to have been there all along, thriving in forgotten spaces, waiting for its turn to bare its teeth. The question asked of us – and that we now turn to our readers – is not *what would you do if it came for you?* but a much more haunting *how sure are you that it hasn't arrived?*

As we checked under our beds and shone lights in our wardrobes, we've come to realise something quite important about these stories. The beating heart of this collection – the one we could hear pulsing throughout – was not one beating behind the walls in a claim for revenge; it was a thriving, fiercely alive entity that refused to concede defeat.

If darkness has many names, its opposition is just as resourceful – the characters in this collection are just as willing to grow claws and fight for themselves. Nothing is a final barrier – not death, not natural disasters, not the upheaval of the world as we know it. Each time, they find a way to keep moving against the fading of light – sometimes through magic, sometimes technology, and often through offering yourself the love denied by those around you. From quiet epiphanies to building whole new realities, all paths are taken to escape the shadows.

And so many times in these stories, we found that those fighting the darkness found the compassion to reach out to those who hadn't been able to fight – from estranged loved ones to creatures of legend – which is maybe where the heart of this collection really lies, in our relentless capacity for connection, and the power it holds.

It has been both amazing and terrifying to follow so many lurking threats for Another Name for Darkness, and we truly appreciate the opportunity to keep on doing it for as long as you'll have us! To every single writer that shared their story, to the booksellers, to the Arts Council, to all of our readers – thank you!

Out into the dark we go once more, and we hope you'll follow.

THE STORIES

CONTENT WARNINGS

*Please be advised that discussions of death,
grief and sexuality may be present
throughout the book.*

Buried Deep: aftermath of a natural disaster;

The Lanky Skin-and-Bones Lady: injury detail, self-harm,
harrassment (mentioned);

A Walking Wound: sexual abuse (referenced), violence;

Moth{er}: child neglect, mental distress, gaslighting, insects;

Coffee: sexual assault (implied), violent death (implied);

The Brother Lorax: unspecified climatic disaster,
death of children (mentioned), weapons;

The Woodworker: child neglect, car accident (mentioned);

Encore: car accident, injury detail;

A Cut Rock Does Not Bleed, It Shines: injury detail,
mental distress, disordered eating.

On this home by Horror haunted—tell me truly, I implore—
Is there—is there balm in Gilead?—tell me—tell me, I implore!
Quoth the Raven "Nevermore."

– THE RAVEN,
Edgar Allan Poe

Each man's death diminishes me,
For I am involved in mankind.
Therefore, send not to know
For whom the bell tolls,
It tolls for thee.

– FOR WHOM THE BELL TOLLS,
John Donne

BURIED DEEP

Seán Finnan

What a different earth I am faced with. Occasionally it catches me and momentarily I am breathless. A feeling of faintness comes over me. Dread and absolute panic. I tell myself to calm down, that things change. The important thing is to remain calm. The sun just dries the crust. The smell of early summer is gone and replaced now by the must of sodden decomposition, of wet clay. Spring came before winter this year. I watched the shoots of daffodils wither from the freak frost on Christmas morning, the ground outside flaked with the delicate white flowers of blackthorn, falling like cold ashes upon the grass's fresh growth. Our first winter of loss. All buried beneath. If it was the first spring that claimed them, it was the second spring that condemned us. Nothing ever lets me forget. I watch a robin come to earth, sit on the mound of dirt before me, and chirp this almost freakish air. I hear it when I close my eyes. Daily she comes. The same habit. Stops her song, flicks her head in my direction before plucking an earthworm from the soft brown ground. Lifts off. Swirls around in the bare brutish sky before coming back to earth. Gravitates towards where the hedge that held her nest should be. Will scratch the ground, attempt to feed the chicks that rest beneath, to keep being a mother, providing for the progeny that are no longer there. On another day, I watched a blue tit fly straight into the ground, as a cormorant would dive into the open ocean. Death on impact. Warm in my hands I turned it over. Small black eyes open and lifeless, its pale yellow feathers had already turned grey. I told Lar what I had witnessed and he just grunted at me. Nothing new there. This constant silence is my penance of some sort. A punishment. If you hear the thunder knocking on your roof in the future, take it from me, it is a war cry. Make no mistake. We'd gotten too comfortable. We turned up the TV. The weather presenter said red alert. Lar poured me another glass of wine, laughed and browsed Netflix. The rain hit the sun window with the ferocity of shells pulsing from an automatic gun. God, you'd think that might have been a warning. Instead it was as soothing as any sedative. I drifted away on the couch.

I sometimes wonder what it would be like to perform an exorcism on the earth. Whether archaeology is a form of it. The act of digging into the ground, the expulsion of objects hidden beneath it, resurfacing things that, like demons, occupy our present, begin to taunt it. Can you really read love in such things? Whether people loved as they do now, in sickness and in health, until death did them apart? What if, I think, inside, this man is already dead? When someone is no longer present, when each day they drift further inwards, obsess over loss, at the injustice of it all, where do you go? Dig deep now and uncover the past that you have lost.

'Dig,' he says to me again.

I take the weathered shovel from Lar's calloused hands. I catch his eyes looking at me for one bare second, searching for something. His beard, its own bird's nest, can no longer hide the gauntness of his face; the contours of his cheeks map a territory that feels alien, distant, no longer mine.

What if I can never bring him back? This resentment just builds and builds. Everything that he has ever worked for one day gone. Like salt in water. Tasting it only in bitter memory.

His hands are already red raw, while mine are chaffed, cold and pink.

The robin is still picking at the ground. Seagulls look down upon us as they pass by. All of us in unfamiliar landscapes. I feel a thud of guilt as the earth slaps against the ground. This morning I told him I loved him. Pressed my hand into his. He asked me to turn up the radio, then grew frustrated that we'd only made the news on one miserable day.

'Nobody cares.'

You got that right.

Was the venom always there? Percolating slowly and eventually saturating his mind and body. Or was it one of these things that just needed a catalyst, a big event to set the spark? Do some people cope while others grow? Do some become scapegoats while others saints, some mopping up the blame so that others drift through memory without a blemish? Didn't I push him?

13

Try to move her on from the mantlepiece? Scatter them, man, I said to him when all around us the trees budded green slips, while the remaining blood orange petals of our tulips closed rank around the stigma. We can make it special. His mother was never fussy, never deigned to specify. I offered to drive. Anywhere you want to go to, Lar. Cliffs of Moher. Lough Ree. The Camlin if needs be. The right moment may never come.

A split second.

Now where is she?

Buried beneath.

And what am I left with?

These thoughts.

Every memory of the past double-edged, open to being interpreted anew. My own worst interrogator. Always on search for a new meaning. Distrustful of my answers. Burying deeper. To prove to myself, perhaps, that the evidence was always there.

'I'll protect you,' he said, and grabbed me in close. I said I'd never heard such thunder.

'It's like the clouds are angry.'

'What are we doing here, anthropomorphising the clouds like primaeval runts,' he says, his teeth a purple hue from the wine.

I tell him to go fuck himself or words to that effect.

'It's only thunder,' he said, clapping his hands together. 'Air meeting air.'

The lights flickered before the darkness. The kitchen sink belched raw sewage. A neighbour's roar. The rain fell in a tumult and the earth expanded. Lar cried out from the window.

Dear Lord, what might have happened if I hadn't scrambled? Just grabbed her there from the mantlepiece. Lugged the vase under my arm. Followed his request. Perhaps all might have been forgiven. Perhaps we might be partners now, soldiers trudging through the tough times. It takes a crisis to know love, they say. Is this it? Do I know now?

'Dig,' he says, looking up from the pit, the earth mounded around him. Sweat bubbling upon his forehead. 'Dig.'

The words have become a refrain.

Dig.

Dig.

Dig.

A split second decision, I tell myself. Not even. A fraction of that. Maybe even less than a TENTH. Basic instinct, Lar, that's all it was. Nothing else. Just plain old basic instinct. Survival. System override. The need to GET THE FUCK OUT OF THERE NOW.

I pierce the blade into the earth, the surface crusted, the ground beneath sodden. The earth groans. I think of the depths we have to reach and I too sigh in solidarity. He pants beside me. A man who has never worked a manual gig in his life. Watch him scramble with a bobbin to tie his hair out of his face. Whisper words beneath his breath. Above us splinter thick clouds of slate blue. Shafts of sunlight dart through the fissures and begin to illuminate the pit, the hole, the layers of dirt. The ground is a swell of mushy peat, a fibrous mishmash of twigs and roots. Entrails of heather too, some still with their dainty lilac flowers. The ground creaks and gurgles like a baby. Sucks too like a newborn grasping at their mother's teat. I feel it latch onto my shovel. I pull. It resists. I pull again. This newborn land drinks deep. Thirst evident all around us. Half consumed trees spat out upside down. Nothing left of them but gangly sinewy roots, like the perished hands of the drowned grasping towards the cold and callous air. Telephone poles snapped and swallowed. Fences and sheds engulfed whole by the roaming sod. Our home then. Nothing more than one last bitter aperitif.

Day after day we have come here. Ever since. The man can't even speak about it. Has barely said one word. I try and coax him. To speak about what has happened. How else can we move on? How else can we begin to once again pick up the pieces of our lives? The only thing right now that can animate him is his shovel. Barely eating, he's more and more resembling a flagpole, his black hair waving in the wind, a marker stuck into this barren land. This whole thing is lunacy. Too much happening in my head all at once, I fuck the shovel against the ground. Glare at him. Challenging him to say something.

He doesn't appreciate the gesture.

Mutters something beneath his breath.

Resorted now to the primitive, communicating with me through words that have yet to trouble themselves with a second syllable. I ignore this burgeoning chasm of silence.

16

Shrugging it off has become second nature. I grab my phone and scroll through stories.

Ghosts of past lives light up my screen; on summer holidays, cocktails under orange sunsets, keys turned on freshly painted front doors. My fingers type "die bitch" beneath each one. Then up it pops. Again. Yes. Again.

An exclamation mark encased within a red triangle.

Not good.

Not good at all.

I glance towards himself and say, 'Another storm on the way.'

Silence.

'Could be another.'

What's the word again.

'A deluge,' I mutter to myself, doing my best to mimic a feeling of cool composure.

And what do I get in return? Niente. The dumb waiter himself gaping at air like a suffocating goldfish.

'We're talking status red here, Lar,' my voice, involuntarily, raising a notch.

His shovel snaps through fibre. The sun winks off a turbine's swirling blade. The cuckoo's mocking cry could not fill this void between us.

'Lar,' I hiss.

He pushes his long black hair from his eyes, wipes his dirt-ridden face with his T-shirt. Sweating away in his white cotton top and blue denim jeans, thinking he's working the railroads or some shit. Slugs greedily from a battered plastic bottle of water. Personally now, my mercury levels are rising. Nobody and I mean nobody, not even Mother Teresa could be that absorbed in their work.

Need I remind you *Lar* that what we experienced was, dare I say it, an Act of God!

God, Lar.

God.

And Mrs. FBD, kitted out in her purple double-decker suit was *crystal clear* about that. A God damned Act of God. Meaning, my dear, that this whole *situation* was, dare I say it, outside of human control. There are some things that, believe it or not, surpass even my own most humble abilities. An Act of God, if you can circle this particular square Lar, is one of them. Yes. That's right. I, Alison, was powerless before the careless acts of a wanton divinity. Was not in fact omnipresent. Was in fact helpless. Totally inept. Pure useless.

'Dig.'

He mumbles this word between the gulps of water. Cooing to himself more than me. Keeping his sanity on side. Mine at bay. His grave is getting deeper. Clay and peat pile up. Notifications light up my phone asking me whether I am ok, whether I need help. DMs saying Alison Alison oh if there's anything I can do just say.

Fuck off. Fuck off. Fuck off.

He stops then. Hits pause. Looks at me from a distance, considers my presence. Shadows pass over his face. I know what's coming. Same thing he has said again and again and again.

You.

Were.

Right.

Be-side.

Her.

I can feel my heart jerking, my whole body about to spasm in defence.

'I just can't believe it,' he utters. 'You literally just left her there.'

That's because *my precious* I was, you know, too focused on fucking living to worry about the dead. I don't say this. Never have. I dance instead around the sensitivities of a grieving son.

'How many times,' I plead. 'How many times do we have to go through this.'

I sometimes feel I am going mad. Man is traumatised. Stuck. Not able to go on, we spin daily on this merry-go-round of blame.

'There was a LITERAL landslide,' I say, pointing to the stubby hill in the distance. 'From up there.'

He glares at me. Shakes his head.

'A bog slide actually,' he says. 'It's not the same thing.'

Words momentarily escape me.

'A bog slide,' he continues, 'is *actually* much slower than a landslide.'

'Is it,' I say.

'Yes,' he says. 'You're making it sound way more dramatic than it was.'

'Lar,' I say, my voice quiet now with seething, volcanic rage. 'Our house is literally buried beneath us. Tell me again how I am making things *dramatic.*'

I point at the hill beyond that's half gone, turbines still sticking up straight while the once green fields, fir forests, and farms have been scraped clean from the slopes, before settling

upon us, the estate built in the bog hole, delightfully christened as Prospect Meadows. Lar shakes his head like a sullen
child. Refuses to deal with reality. I point to the hill again.

'That hill over there. Gouldry or whatever the fuck it's
called. Guess what. We're actually standing on it.'

I jump up and down with the intention of reinforcing my
point.

'Right here, Lar. Right here.'

He turns his back and adopts his Mother Teresa I'm so
holy I don't make mistakes aura, picks up his shovel, and continues to deepen this gaping hole between us.

This daily toil has turned my thoughts as fetid as the land
around me. I can't shake this feeling that he regrets surviving.
I carry it around like an anvil in my stomach. That he feels we
could have accomplished more being swallowed by the earth
than the existence we now have. That our domestic bliss could
all still be preserved down below like pickled beetroot in a
sanitised jar. Our one opportunity to become immortal. Like
the Old Croghan man. He might have had his head chopped
off but his body, halved as it was, lived to tell the whole story. The midland's own Pompeii. I'll show you eternity in the
Pompeii man's endless wank. Should have handcuffed you to
the bed. Straddled you there and then. We'd live forever just
as you dreamed. Edging toward oblivion. Peat pounding at the
door. Sludging through the windows. Grinding up and down.
Star crossed lovers that would give future archaeologists

renown the world over. Might have been a nice way to end things. Live a second life of infamy. Create a new narrative. The midlands? Repressed? God no? No last rites here. They fuck in the face of...

Thunder.

I look up to the sky at the thickly stitched clouds condemned to yet another battle in this endless elemental war. Crows caw and flee. I feel naked, exposed. The day grows dark. I want to leave. To go. To just go. Bodies are meant to be buried. He wants to take something back that is no longer his. I can already hear his cruel laugh ring around my head at the thought of telling him this. Some things are better left unsaid. I laugh thinking about it now. The long months in hospice. Radiators on full blast. The skin on her hand paper-thin and cold yet gripping my hand with delicate force. Look after him. And when I'm gone scatter me with the wind. I honestly think she'd understand our situation. Would find it quite nice being buried in our home. Like her own private mausoleum. The woman had a sense of humour. Something I only wish was hereditary.

I feel the first heavy drop of rain. The crows have departed. The cuckoo has quietened. Stillness spreads. I consider going back to the hotel but immediately rule it out. Too much like the valley of squinting windows for my liking. Every gesture a judgement, every word an expired voucher of charity. I fight so hard to not think about anything. To not consider what I have lost. What I still have hanging over me. My future is underneath the ground and what Lar can't reckon with, what I am struggling to communicate to him is it's gone. It's all in the past now. Dig as deep as you like you can never recover what we once had. Never mind your mother. What was it we once had? Domestic bliss? Comfort? Walls secure and stable enough to start a family, to grow old, create roots, and watch them flourish. Did we actually have that? It wasn't just a dream?

I stroll on the crust of this lunar plain, look for signifiers, some markers that will reassure me, will say this is still your home. But all are silent. The hill still stands, its presence haunting, a glitch, feeding my unease that it remains while all else has changed. Two silver birches sway solemnly against one another, at the far ebb of the landslide, condemned to rely on the support of each other and no longer the land they were planted in. A solitary telephone pole stands erect, still proudly hanging on to an election poster of our local councillor, as it swivels on one nail. His words of empty solace on local radio in the aftermath still echo in my ears.

'And this, as they say now, is an awful tragedy, an unfortunate tragedy, but it's something now that we're unlikely to see the likes now of again,' he said, on Shannonside's early morning breakfast show.

The presenter, fair play to her, asked him about the turbines. About whether or not they should have received planning permission. Whether or not it was a good idea to construct a wind farm on what was basically an upland bog. Whether or not the farm owners would be liable for damages, and whether the homeowners would get amnesty from their mortgage repayments.

'Sarah Sarah Sarah,' he said to the presenter. 'These Acts of God...'

Those words.

We encounter them everywhere. A magic reprieve that forever postpones any blame, any action, any accountability.

Yesterday.

In FBD. In her nice little office. Her double-decker purple suit. A bobble-headed radio presenter nodding on her desk in the draught of her small desk fan. I dragged him to the office. She was perched over her table, ruffling through the papers of our claim. Her nails were lilac. A morning shellac. A Swarovski bracelet with a Minnie Mouse figure made from diamond hung from her wrist, swinging like a pendulum every time she moved her hand to gesticulate. All hands this woman was.

'With this being an Act of God,' she said, swinging her hand in a flourish as if talking about the cosmic birth of the solar system.

Could feel him beside me simmering like a copper kettle.

Squeezing his hand.

'We can't because...'

Act of God.

Hand flourish

'I'm sorry because...'

Act of God.

Hand flourish

'There's nothing we can do because...'

Act of God.

Hand flourish

'We're very very...'

Act of God.

23

Hand flourish

'If we had to cover every...'

Act of God.

'You can understand our...'

'ACT OF GOD,' screamed Lar.

That was it then. No point intervening now. Couldn't ever let her away with an expression that is actually *baked* into the lexicon of the industry.

'Have you not got the fucking memo,' he screamed. 'GOD IS DEAD HONEY.'

Her face went then. White as a sheet. Carte blanche as the French say. Lips pursed like burst bilberries.

'I'm sorry,' she said, walking to the door in short spurting strides, opening it wide then as if to say GET THE FUCK OUT NOW.

Which we did. Rather sharply.

I've long ago ran out of tears. I sleep in short spurts and dream sometimes of home, of childhood. Last night I dreamt of the blue tit twitching in my hands. It smiled at me. For a moment there was something between us. She buried her head into the palm of my hand. I felt warm for a moment. Then I woke up. Pale sunlight streaked in through the grimy net curtains, the thin walls barely muffled the morning radio show in a room next door and Lar was already up, had left and gone to the restaurant for breakfast by himself. His car keys sparkled on the stained chipwood surface of the locker and for a moment I thought of grabbing the few belongings I owned and driving somewhere, anywhere, far away from here. Yet the promises I've made to other people outweigh any of the promises I've made to myself.

The rain now falls in a thick flurry, washing these cold memories away. The birch trees groan against one another. The roots creak, as the wind turns gale force, conjuring new sounds out of this boggy plain. A fork of lightning reveals the cracks in the porcelain-pink sky above me. Thunder moans. The ground below me softens and stews. My heart quickens. I can feel it happening again. I rush back through the bog, wary of craters, the soft wet ground that at any moment can catch my footing, bring me to earth, engulf me. I see the remnants of the hole in the mounds of dirt circling it, like melting glaciers now, the earth liquifying and seeping slowly back towards the pit. Lar is about seven foot deep at this stage. I peer into the hole. It looks like a festered wound. Lar in the middle of it, dirt-ridden and bloody, up to his knees in a pungent brown broth.

'We have to go,' I beg. 'You're asking for it if you stay here any longer.'

Nothing.

'Now,' I plead. 'The car is started. I can run you a bath in the hotel. We can have a drink. I'll treat us to dinner. Just come.'

He casts a sharp glance towards me, his face gaunt as a skeleton.

'So close,' he says, his mouth white with dehydration, barely enough spittle left to mouth those words. I look down at him now as he pummels the shovel at the ground.

'Lar,' I say gently, trying a different tactic. 'We'll come back tomorrow. We'll get help.'

He continues at the task in front of him. Has tied cloth around his hands, an attempt to stem the flow of blood from seeping through the abrasions on his palms. The blood mingles with the dirt of his arms, flows freely into this cauldron of madness. He hits the shovel against the ground. Whimpers in pain, lets go of the shovel, and gazes up at me.

'Alison,' he says, as if seeing me now for the first time.

'Lar,' I say, hunching down. 'Come on now.'

He looks up at me and smiles.

'We're so close, love,' he says. 'We're nearly home.'

Tears run down his bloodshot eyes. Then, in one swift action, his hand has grasped my ankle. I feel his callouses rough against my skin. I scream as he pulls. Stumble then and slip. Cold clammy wetness runs down my back, water soaks into my shoes, head aches from the fall. Roots poke out through the pit's sludgy sides, graze the back of my neck. The cold fingers of death herself. My body shivers. With anger. White rage. My two fists slam into Lar's chest. He takes the blows until I tire.

'You rotten bastard,' I whimper when I'm finished.

He pulls me in close, puts his arms around me. A hand upon my head.

'I'm sorry,' he says. 'I'm really sorry.'

I push him off from me.

'Please, Ali,' he says, taking the rags off and showing me his bloody, bruised and swollen hands. 'I need you. I can't do it anymore.'

Yellow puss seeps from the abrasions on his palms. His fingers swollen to the size of sausages.

'You promised me,' I whimper.

My teeth chatter. Feet going numb in the cold water. The rain brings the curtains down early on the day while the earth above us continues to dilute.

It flows.

It moves.

It falls.

I've the very real fear of the walls caving in, of not being able to get back out again. 'We're still a team. We're still Alila,' he whispers into my ear.

I feel the earth clotting my hair, dribbling down my face, caking my clothes. This feeling of being buried alive. Slow suffocation. I no longer can tell who I am anymore. What we want. Where we are going.

'It just needs to be cracked,' he says, his fingers pointing at the pool of brackish water rising beneath us.

'What does?'

'Our sun window,' he smiles. 'And *you* said we couldn't afford it at the time.'

A finger pokes me in the chest. Followed by the blade of the shovel pushed into my hand. I take it. Not sure what else to do. Pluck it from his bleeding hands. I grip the cold metal tightly along its heel, look toward Lar, at his large lunar eyes. Raise the blade high as if I'm conducting some type of sacrificial offering. Slam it hard against the ground. It bounces back with venom. I feel the window beneath us quiver. Lar claps me on the back.

'Again,' he says. 'Harder.'

I go again. Again and again, harder with every hit until my arms are heavy and my hands are numb. He grips my shoulders tightly, shouting words of encouragement in my ear, words marinated by the tumult all around us. Eventually it cracks. I shatter the shards from the frame as the murky water, along with my fears of trench foot, empties from the pit and into the darkness. We stand and gaze below us, at this poky entrance into the underworld. Listen to the dull echo of falling water reverberate upwards from the cavernous darkness.

'Honey,' he says, shaking his head in disbelief. 'We're some team.'

The horrors of the previous months fold back upon themselves. It's all there. In the darkness beneath. The opportunity to forget that these months ever happened, to go back in time and pick up where we left off. How many others could have this opportunity? My heart flutters at the thought of never having to see those threadbare and moth-infested curtains in that stinking hotel room again.

He lowers himself first through the window. I hear a thud as he hits the floor.

This is it I think. This is all we have.

I scramble through the window.

Each other.

I fall.

The carpet squelches as I land two feet on the upper landing. A darkness so complete I feel adrift in space. My hands search for a form.

'Lar,' I whisper. 'Lar.'

A voice comes at me from the dark.

'Over here.'

I feel a hand upon me.

Things scurry above us. Soft clicking. Beetles maybe. Cockroaches. God knows what. The smell is rancid, of bitter earth.

'My phone is dead. Yours?'

A light emerges, waging a feeble battle against the darkness. Lar smiles at me. He mouths the word. I shake my head. He says it louder. No, I say. Look. Look around you. Pale yellow wallpaper we had only put up. Now look at it. I want to. All draped down upon itself. Look closer. Families of beetles feeding off its gluey underside. Spores of fungus glow against the torch's glare. A greeny blue phosphorescence breathes. Eyes. Hundreds of them. Glaring at us. We are trespassers in our own home.

'Lar,' I whisper.

My voice catches. Barely audible.

'Turn it off.'

Feel safer in the darkness. No longer under observation.

'Two secs,' says Lar, pulling my face towards his, a soft kiss on my cold cheek. 'Let me check if downstairs is safe.'

Oh how kind of you, Lar.

His feet squelch as he walks down the carpeted stairs, two steps at a time, toward the living room, toward his beloved mother in the clay vase upon the mantlepiece. Above me, I hear the thunder roar once more, bellowing its commands to the earth. To continue to drink. And it does, past its saturation point, oozing like effluence, the waste of millennia streaming through the broken window. I don't move. For some reason

I no longer feel scared. All my anxiety, my stress, my worry abandoning me.

I stay still, standing under the deluge, under the falling bog. I feel the peat enmesh my hair, mask my face, and trickle between the crevices of my clothes. I feel it running, seeping down the stairs, onto the tiled kitchen floor. Completing its work. His voice echoes at me as if travelling through water.

'Ali,' he says, his voice creaking with emotion. 'I have her.'

It washes over me as the earth continues embalming me, gifting me this new skin.

'A celebration,' he shouts.

How long before this place fills up with the cascading earth?

I hear press doors slamming open. Slamming shut.

'I see some of us were thinking ahead,' he roars. 'Red or white?'

But I have stopped listening. The cold peat is beginning to engulf me. All feels still now. A cold calm tranquillity washes over me under this earth. I feel it covering my eyes, plastering my face. I am becoming clay. I wonder how this bog will preserve me. Whether it will find my shape in this interminable darkness. My true shape. Or whether it will sculpt me anew, towards a form I no longer recognise. Or perhaps it will preserve me in all my bitterness, in all my loss, in all my longing. This shape of me that he and I have sculpted.

ASH BARK

Die Booth

On the day the boys are born, the heavens open. Rain sheets down from rumbling yellow clouds, curtaining the evening dark as night and swilling the day's dust away in a crackle of static. Twin howls drown in the downpour. Twin houses, side by side. A baby born in each, minutes apart, the first roaring into the world head-first and the other following faithfully after. Leo coos at the boom and crack of thunder. Steven, as though he can sense the future, starts to cry.

Their mothers plant trees before the boys are a month old. While the babies kick and wriggle on a blanket on the grass, Rose pats down the mud around an ash seedling. Anne buries an acorn by its side, pressing a blown kiss onto the earth with her fingertips and a wish.

Children grow more quickly than trees, at least for the first couple of years. The boys blossom: one fair, one dark; one sickly, one strong. Steven is bright, Leo sharp-toothed and faithless and brave, both shooting up as their saplings sprout leaves and struggle through their first winters, opening green hearts to the smile of spring.

After that, it evens out. Ash trees grow quicker, but they're smaller. Oaks grow slowly, but if they make it to maturity, they can reach 60 feet. When Leo's oak is five years old, it stands about eight feet tall. Steven's ash sways, yearning cloudwards with slender stems, barely bigger than Anne as she raises her axe. A neat split, right down the trunk. The halves bow out beneath their own weight, bleeding sap. Anne taps a wooden wedge into the gap with the back of the axe head.

'That'll hold,' she says. 'Hand him over.'

Rose unwraps Steven from his blanket. Passes him, naked, pale and frail as crocus stems, through the split in the ash to Anne. The morning dew still drenches the grass, the sun not yet come up. Leo watches silently with big solemn eyes, Steven too weak to even shiver. They pass him through three times, as the horizon starts to spill silver with dawn's shine. Rose's lip quivers, but Anne wears a blank mask of determination. As Rose wraps Steven back up warm, resting his head against her shoulder, Anne knocks out the wedge from the trunk and picks up a coil of baling wire.

'Put your back against that.'

Rose leans on the tree, covering Steven's pale face with her palm as Anne wraps the wire around the split halves and winds it tight, shouldering her own half until the trunk is cinched together again with haybands. Leo braces tiny hands against the bark as she twists the last end off. She ruffles his hair. Says, 'Good job.'

'Thank you,' Rose says.

'Now we wait.' Anne shrugs, but she presses a careful hand to Rose's shoulder as she passes, fleeting and strong as hope.

The ash tree grows back, sheltered by the oak. It heals with the same long scar that Steven has down his chest.

'I'll have a scar even bigger one day.' Leo says, openly envious always of this thing of which Steven is so shy.

'What from?' Steven asks, his voice wobbling.

'From fighting a bear,' Leo says, with conviction. He slashes the drowsy summer air with the stick he's carrying like a sword. Noting Steven's expression he says, 'Don't worry. I'll win. I'll beat him, and he's a bad bear.'

Steven, standing in the swishing shallows of the stream, shades his eyes as Leo wades to the middle, steps sure. 'I don't want you to bleed.'

The dancing water chuckles up around Leo's knees, steeping the hem of his shorts. Steven looks down at his scar, pale skin beginning to pink in the sun. Leo says, 'I won't bleed. I'm too brave.' He says, 'You didn't, either. They opened you up like a treasure chest and put an acorn where your heart was.'

Steven squints at him in the sunlight, hair a halo of gold, and starts to giggle. Leo is a shadow in the current, cool and sheltering. His laugh sounds like bubbles. 'Treasure chest,' Steven says, feeling all big and shiny inside. He searches in his pocket, pulls out a copper coin. 'Here. Happy birthday.' It's not their birthday, but he holds it out, offering. Leo grins. Produces his own coin, preciously collected pocket money.

'Come on. Take it. Swap.' Leo inches back. 'Happy birthday to us!'

Taking a step further, unsteady pebbles underfoot, Steven follows him into the deep waters.

At seventeen, Steven's still scared of storms. He can't explain it away, except that the lash of lightning makes him feel like his bones might crack. Then, the drum of the rain against his window panes turns into a tune, a rhythm too regular to be only the sound of the squall, the shadow cast on his curtains too big to be just the thrashing trees outside. Pulling aside the drapes, he sees Leo's laughing face.

'Not in the storm, you idiot!'

Climbing over the sill, Leo flicks rain-black curls out of his eyes and smiles. 'Let me in quicker next time, then.'

'It's bad enough when you do it in the dry,' Steven says, but his complaint holds no heat. He knows and Leo knows that Steven's impressed when Leo climbs the ivy between their windows to sneak into Steven's room.

'I won't fall,' Leo says. His eyes are dark and bright, like lightning in a night sky.

You will, Steven thinks.

One timid, one bold. That winter brings snow. Even the stream freezes over on top, its secret song subdued beneath a fragile glazing of ice. They shuffle booted footsteps down the lane, skidding and yelping, Steven steadying his skating flails against Leo's arm.

'It's cold.' The tip of Leo's nose is rosy above his red scarf. He sounds grumpy. There are snowflakes in his hair. Steven raises a hand to brush them away, then can't: they're stars in a clear sky, for a moment, melting. Steven's heart is melting with them.

'I'll warm you up,' he says. 'Give me your hands.' The snow muffles the hedgerows. Across the field, their trees are cloaked in it, sharing a single blanket. The air is crystal, sharp and clear. Silent, so only the fogged cloud of their breath mingling shows that time hasn't stopped altogether. Without words, Steven eases the glove from Leo's left hand, fingers curled palm-up. Cradles it. Turns it over to examine carefully, and Leo lets him. Square nails. The delicate pathway of lines on his palm. Steven traces one with a fingertip, all the way to the stuttering pulse in Leo's bare wrist, and Leo shivers, breathing out a tiny almost-sound in a puff of heat. A hot thrill rushes beneath Steven's skin. Just his hand, yet that bared palm cradles Steven's patchwork heart; his blood turns to steam. He presses a kiss to Leo's palm, smelling the ghost of coal tar soap. Then Leo's fingers are cupping his cheek, drawing him in, and his pulse leaps like he missed a stair, and when their lips meet it is warm.

'Avoid an ash, it counts the flash,' Leo's grandpa Albert used to say. Anne would shush him and Steven had always wondered, as a child, why. When he got older, and asked his mum, Rose told him that the Lightning Tree wasn't unlucky, it was magical. The ability to draw lightning to it was powerful, she said, and special. A special kind of powerful magic, even for boys who are afraid of storms.

When Steven hears the news, he feels nothing but numb. Like the world is carrying on and he's the one who has stopped, frozen.

'It should have been me.'

Rose blinks at him through a film of tears. She says, 'I'm glad it wasn't,' and Steven has the terrifying urge to strike her. His feet thunder up the stairs, but alone in his room all he can see is his own wretched reflection in the closed window that will never again frame a wicked lovely face, waiting to be let inside.

Fire doesn't cleanse. It just destroys. Leo's heart gave out at twenty-two, dead in his bed at the very moment lightning snapped electric fingers, pointing at its prize, and struck the young oak next to the Lightning Tree.

Steven's heart is split in two, yet he's alive.

It should have been him.

He doesn't go to the funeral.

On that day the air stands still. The birds cease singing. The only sound is the crunch of his footsteps like a funeral march. A scent of ice-edged damp, the next year waiting with breath held. It's a glassy day. Brittle. Colourless. Leo isn't in the cemetery, not really, not with its neat white regiments of stones like office cubicles for the gone. He's here in the woody wild. Stolen in the night, heart-struck for loving too truly.

'I loved you, completely, and I love you still and evermore.' Frost soaks into the knees of Steven's trousers as he kneels on scattered twigs and his eyes flood hot. The shattered trunk is white in the quiet mild winter light, its insides outside. Fallen to the right, like even in death it was protecting the little ash shivering at its side. 'It should have been me.' He strokes a palm full of emptiness across the fallen tree, but it won't even give him a splinter.

The leaves change colour. Spotted yellow white green brown. Steven's bed feels like a grave, but he hauls himself out, fingers cramped around the coin in his jacket pocket. The outdoors air is fragrant with damp, rich mud, with dying foliage. The carpet of chestnut russet gives the woods a red glow. When he reaches their trees, the dropped leaves look more like a patchwork quilt. Steven sits. Pats the fallen trunk sinking softly into mossy decline, tucks it in.

'Happy birthday to us.' His voice is a whisper. He uses a chunk of branch to knock the coin into the trunk. It's harder than it looks. His ash tree leans to watch, dripping berries like blood. By the time his brow is sweaty he leans back to see: copper glinting in the dipping light of the sun, precious and precarious as the shadows stretch.

As the years fold, the roots of his tree breach ground, reach up and twine around the capsized branches of his dead love, cradling it in grace. The copper coin becomes a line, winking like bright eyes, seven in a row. Steven learns to bring a hammer to birthday parties, and wonders when the ache will fade. There's a rainbow in the grey bark of his ash: yellow green pink blue, all the colours of sunset pastel, glittering like pearl, like opal; it scintillates like labradorite. Jamming a thumbnail beneath a piece of bark, he picks till it bleeds, pulling off a slice. Does the tree hurt, or does he? It's not a page on which to write legibly, but he writes it all the same, digging the metal nib of his pen in, cramming the words from his fevered brain onto the smooth reverse of the bark. 'Please reply,' he says. Lays the letter on the oak. Leaves it to rot and take its message across the veil.

Steven dreams.

Colours and heat, words without meanings and feelings without words, stirred in an almost-remembered haze, until in that time between oblivion and rising, Leo is there and says, 'Don't wait for me.' Steven frowns, wobbling on the tightrope of sleep. And there's his smile and bright lovely eyes, so familiar Steven can taste his lips on the edge of waking, and so out of reach. 'Live for us,' Leo says. 'Live for me.'

Life, like a stream, does not stay in one place, not even if you want it to. A stream flowing is never still: even if it looks motionless, even if it's trapped in ice, there's movement, pulling below the surface, surging always onwards.

On a Tuesday morning in June, a girl in the typing pool smiles at Steven as he squeaks past with the mail cart. Her name is Carol and her blonde hair glitters in a crispy hair-spray halo that he wants to stroke his fingers over like a plasma globe. On Friday, they go to The Trooper and split the bill on chicken in a basket and black forest gateaux. The cherries taste like lipstick, and her lipstick tastes of cherries. As the rear window steams up in his Ford Escort his heart cracks and mends, cracks and mends.

Life passes. It is happy.

When the trunk of the oak holds eleven coins, Steven marries Carol in May. The confetti smells of sugar, stamped in little rice paper shapes of bells and doves and hearts in all the colours of a pastel sunset. It flutters in the air like snowflakes and for a breath of a second Steven pictures it glittering like stars in a sweep of dark curls.

At thirteen coins, Kevin is born. Steven holds him to his heartbeat and smells his hair. Blonde, like both his parents. Steven knows he's just imagining it, but his scar aches, like there's something inside, pushing, too big and precious to be contained in his chest.

Eighteen, and Eleanor enters their lives, a summer baby just like her brother. The years stack up like loose change, easily spent. Steven remembers, and he forgets, but mostly it's just there, ever-present. Like a shadow. Like being watched lovingly over for so long at such a distance that you barely notice any more.

Sometimes, things pull him back into the past. A song. A glimpse of red scarf. A Saturday in September when they stroll into a market and he's surrounded by the scent of coal tar soap, and the expectation of a different hand in his is so strong he staggers with it, running to the public bathroom and staring at his reflection in the mirror trying to recognise anything, *anything*, in those tired eyes.

Life passes. It is happy. But it is long. The gold of his hair turns to ashes, as gold so often does.

He still dreams of dark eyes and laughter. This was no sudden crash and tangle. They grew up together, entwined from the start, the years only tightening their warp and weft, until the storm severed their strands yet left them still drifting together like tangled kite strings. Unmoored, but tied too tightly to unpick those fast knots: even as the years drag their cut fibres further apart, Steven doesn't want to separate them fully. No matter how long the distance, they have held fast. A remembrance. Bows of fraying silk for him to stroke reverently in the quiet privacy of memory. If he were to untie them now, he might unravel; a split ash tree with its bindings cut, falling apart and never healing.

Life passes.

They all move on – his wife, children, grandchildren – swimming the rushing stream of time, waving their goodbyes. Great grandchildren are as familiar as strangers, names on a Christmas card list, too awkward to get close to. Because Steven is still alive, huddling around the flame of his memories.

It's been a long time since he visited in spring. So long he can't recall. The warmth of the evening sun touches him like a hand on his shoulder as he walks the path to the spreading ash. It takes him longer than he remembers, the track rutted up in footprints dried into the last rainfall's mud, his bag weighty across back.

The ash tree waves raised branches in the breeze, confetti-ing petals as white as his hair, as white as snowflakes. Beautiful, but carrying the scent of death. When Steven reaches it, he leans against the trunk, greets it like a friend, as he catches his breath.

He's tied to this tree. He can't leave.

In its shadow, the dead oak is full of coins, no space left. The ferryman's toll a thousand times over. Sitting, he strokes a hand across the spiny crests of them, where the glowing prickle of moss waves fronds like tiny ferns, undulating. The sun is going down. He's ready to go home.

The axe is heavy in his hands. He hefts it, weakly. The first chop sends an explosion of crows croaking. It barely makes a split in the bark that long since absorbed the hay bands. Sweat slicks his palms; he readjusts the handle. Perhaps some small part of this tree still longs to fall apart. The second strike is stronger. As night drops softly, Steven hews, shedding the weight of decades in a splintering creak like the crack of lightning, finally.

As it falls, he falls too.

The grass is soft. It's night, but not – dark and bright at once, a starlit dreaming sky. Leo opens his bright dark eyes, and yawns, and smiles. Opens his arms and says, 'Good evening, my love. I missed you.'

In the morning the sun comes out.

Steven isn't there anymore. Just a felled ash tree. Just the shape of a man, lain against the coin-clustered trunk of a dead oak, vacated. Sprouting from his chest is a tiny oak sapling.

THE LANKY SKIN-AND-BONES LADY

Chris Kuriata

When rain flooded Glenridge Valley, my cousin Emy and her family came to stay with us. Uncle Louis had insurance, so he secretly rooted for the house to break away from its foundation and float down the river. Glenridge Valley was an awful place to live, overrun with mosquitoes and soggy soil. Losing their house in a flood would be just what the family needed to start over someplace more hospitable. Of course, my uncle kept his wishes private, not wanting to be seen as "lazy" or "getting something for nothing", which is ridiculous. He worked hard every day at the press shop to afford insurance. Should he feel guilty because he rang the jackpot?

To my delight, Emy slept in my bed. At night, we whispered to one another, trading scary stories, testing our bravery.

'Do you know about the Lanky Skin-and-Bones Lady?' Emy asked.

Only vaguely, things I'd overheard from older girls at school, most of which I didn't understand, but that left me with an uncomfortable sensation, a mixture of disappointment and dizziness.

The Lanky Skin-and-Bones Lady used to live along the escarpment. She went through life giving away whatever people asked of her: her possessions, her home, her dignity. People pounced on her generosity. They asked for things they didn't need, or wound up throwing away. The less she had, the more they demanded.

Even when she'd been stripped of everything, people still asked her to give, and she could only tear off her skin and break off her own bones. Painfully, piece by piece, until she had completely disappeared. The people who swallowed her up didn't even remember her name.

'Let's go outside,' Emy said, reaching for my hand. We left the warmth of our covers to sneak downstairs, tiptoeing so as not to attract the attention of our fathers, who sat in the living room smoking and laughing. They stayed up later than we ever did.

In the garden, green leaves had begun to sprout. They looked so tiny and fragile; I feared a strong wind would demolish the defenceless baby plants. I cringed as Emy walked carelessly through them, unfolding a napkin she'd hidden under her shirt. Inside were scraps saved from dinner: thick chicken skin, and bones covered in rinds of pale fat.

'The Lanky Skin-and-Bones Lady doesn't have her skin or bones anymore, so if you offer her leftovers to build her body back, she'll grant you a wish.'

I don't make wishes. If there is a difference between making a wish and asking for a favour, it eludes me. I dread to think of who I might be asking a favour from, cautious of striking bargains I'll be obligated to hold up.

'How big of a wish will she grant?' I asked. 'If you leave more leftovers, do you get to ask for a bigger wish?'

Emy ignored me. She dumped the contents of the napkin into the garden. I doubted the Lanky Skin-and-Bones Lady had use for cast off table scraps. I didn't believe she stood on the bones of butchered animals, her ribs still smelling of barbeque sauce, her eyes scoops of fat, and her lips gristle. It sounded ridiculous. If the Lanky Skin-and-Bones Lady's only option for becoming whole again was to drape herself in greasy, burnt skin and rotting fat, I didn't think she would have bothered handing out wishes. She would choose to be content with her discorporate state.

Uncle Louis spotted us while he stood outside, urinating through the rungs of the veranda railing. He called us inside, and for the next several hours, Emy and I were forced to empty our father's ashtrays and sing along with their favourite songs. They challenged us to see who could balance a full can of beer atop their head the longest. Only when the orange light of morning warmed the living room did our fathers allow us to take leave and go to bed. We slept for barely twenty minutes before our covers were yanked to the floor by our mothers. Up and at 'em! Sleep deprivation was the punishment for sneaking out. We had no one to blame but ourselves.

Emy's wish came true. The flood water did not recede. The levels rose, and the strong current carried the entire house away. All their clothing and furniture was gone. Uncle Louis danced in the kitchen, spinning joyously, revelling in having lost everything.

I returned to the garden, looking for the spot Emy had cast the skin and bones, but the offering was gone. Even the trampled sprouts had straightened themselves out. Like Uncle Louis, they'd been given the chance to start over.

I remained hesitant the next time someone suggested calling on the Lanky Skin-and-Bones Lady. Trudi and I were selected to stay overnight at the school when a storm broke the windows of the science room. The teacher, Mr. Lillo, worried the classroom would be robbed. He kept all kinds of chemicals locked in the cupboards that could be used to make drugs, or a bomb.

For guard duty, Trudi and I brought sleeping bags to the classroom. We used lanterns to give off light, so any would-be-thieves would see the premises were occupied and be scared off.

I pushed desks together to make a bed, wanting to be above the floor drafts. Unfortunately, with the broken windows, cold air gushed into the room. The papers hanging on the walls lifted, making a constant spattering noise. I don't think it made much difference, sleeping on the desks or the floor. Everywhere in the room, the cold breeze hit you.

'Have you heard of the Lanky Skin-and-Bones Lady?' Trudi asked.

'Kinda, sorta.'

Trudi went to the cupboards we were supposed to be protecting from thieves. Using a tiny screwdriver from her pocket, she removed the door hinges to gain access. Inside were glass jars holding sheep and pig fetuses, suspended in preservation fluid. I stuck my head out of the broken window to avoid the fumes when she opened the jar. The lid groaned. It had likely been holding tight for years.

'What did you wish for?' I asked after Trudi tossed the skin and bones into the bushes beneath the broken window.

'I don't want to be here in the morning. I want to be far away from this town, exhausted, having filled my night with adventure.'

I slept with great difficulty in the cold discomfort of Mr. Lillo's classroom, awakening every hour. I thought I heard a sound from outside, something dragging itself through the bushes. The leaves rattled, and the branches cracked. I closed my eyes, pretending to be asleep. If the Lanky Skin-and-Bones Lady came to take Trudi by the hand and usher her into the night for adventure, I preferred to be left behind.

I woke for good when the janitor arrived to fire up the boiler. The ducts echoed as the walls contracted from the concentrated heat. I didn't want to get out of my sleeping bag. Protecting me from the cold, it felt like armour.

Beside me, Trudi's sleeping bag lay empty. It reminded me of a flattened cocoon, cast away now that its occupant had metamorphosed. Alone, I screwed the hinges back on the cabinet door, and washed the scalpels before Mr. Lillo returned.

No one saw Trudi afterwards. She didn't return to school, but there was nothing unusual about her being absent for days. She didn't spend much time at her parent's house either, so it was possible she'd packed up her clothing and cigarettes and gone somewhere else. According to her friends, she often talked about Vancouver Island, and how one could make a fortune there picking mushrooms.

I found no remains of the lamb fetus in the bushes. Did that mean Trudi was on her way to Vancouver Island, a shovel for picking mushrooms strapped to her back like a prospector, or had she taken the hand of the Lanky Skin-and-Bones Lady, and gone dancing into a never-ending night full of adventure?

For the longest time, I thought the words "coffin" and "casket" were synonyms, but according to Uncle Daniels at the woodwork shop, they described two different styles of final containers.

'The difference is the shape,' he told me while sanding the edges of his latest job. 'A casket has four sides with straight edges, while a coffin has six, with the top angling in.'

'I assume people don't use the word "coffin" anymore because it sounds too ghastly,' I said. 'Dracula sleeps in a coffin. Cigarettes are "coffin nails". It's nicer to be buried in a casket.'

Uncle Daniels blew dust off the smooth edge. 'You might be right, Emery.'

I paid him, and he handed me the tiny wooden coffin, fresh from his lathe. The wood still felt warm from his vigorous sanding. I smelled the heated grain through the linen cloth I wrapped the coffin in to keep it from getting scratched. I paid for the coffin out of my own pocket, but would be reimbursed, plus expenses, when I made the delivery after school.

Uncle Louis was the first to bury a finger outside of the press shop. He lost his index finger in the machine – would have lost the tip of his thumb too, but he managed to fold it in at the last second and escape the hundreds of pounds of pressure from the metal clamp.

If the finger had been recovered immediately, Uncle Louis would have taken the hour-long drive to the hospital in Shipman's Corner, preserving his finger in the icy red cooler the rest of the press shop workers kept their lunchtime beers in. However, because the finger had tumbled deep into the arteries of the machine, it took the men hours to disassemble the whole damn thing and discover its hiding place. They pulled the machine apart in a big hurry and didn't keep track of which screw went where, so putting it back together took several days of trial and error. Uncle Louis said it was a moot point. The recovered finger was all battered out of shape. It looked like a stubbed-out cigarette.

When Uncle Louis finally returned to work, his co-workers presented him with the recovered finger. Grinning, Uncle Louis pressed the finger to his stump, as though the two ends might reconnect like magnets clicking together. The press shop workers all laughed. Uncle Louis knew how to tickle everyone's funny bone.

He had no use for the finger, but didn't want to toss it into the garbage in case the Gods of Accidents got the idea Uncle Louis thought his fingers worthless and decided to relieve him of more.

His first thought was to bury his finger in the garden, but Auntie Pamela grabbed the trowel out of his hand and kicked the dirt back into the hole he'd dug. She hated the idea of any part of him contributing to the nutrients in the soil. She feared he'd poison the vegetables, and all the tomatoes would taste of his cigarettes and brow sweat.

He lost the finger at the press shop, so at the press shop he would bury it. The men all made a good time out of the ceremony. Without being asked, Uncle Daniels built a 2 by 3" coffin for the finger using a strip of oak left over from a dining room table job. The men assembled at the back of the press shop for the burial service. A few of 'em set down their beers long enough to share fond memories of Uncle Louis' finger; the cigars it had tapped, the women it had delighted, and how it would be missed. Afterwards, the boss let 'em knock off a half hour early, so they went to the Brass Boot, where they toasted pints in memory all night long.

Whatever circumstances that led to the amputation of Uncle Jesse's finger a year later must have been embarrassing, because he never revealed them to anyone. Twenty minutes before quitting time, Uncle Jesse hit the kill switch on his machine and walked to the bathroom with his left hand clamped beneath his armpit.

Following Uncle Louis' lead, Uncle Jesse buried his finger behind the shop, hiring Uncle Daniels to build another tiny coffin. With this addition of a second plot, the land out back of the press shop officially became a cemetery.

Uncle Daniels didn't need to be asked to build a coffin when Uncle Dale lost his finger. He got to work as soon as the local gossip carried him the news about the latest press shop mishap. Because he'd been given a strong lead time, Uncle Daniels varnished the wood. Dark as a mug of coffee, the coffin roof reflected the blue sky, making it look like a little pool of water at the bottom of the grave, until Uncle Dale pushed in the dirt and covered it forever.

Uncle Russell envied the bond the missing finger forged between the other men. He felt left out of their four-fingered handshakes. To no one's surprise, Uncle Russell became the fourth member of their crew to lose a piece of his hand in the machine.

'I'm not saying he lost his finger on purpose,' Uncle Louis said.

Uncle Jesse nodded. 'He worked carelessly. Not a man trying to lose a finger, but a man who wouldn't be disappointed if he did.'

After school, when I arrived at the press shop bearing the new coffin, my four uncles were assembled out back, cigarettes dangling from their lips, looking down at the crudely scattered earth from the disinterred graves. The robber left the tiny coffins behind. They lay on their sides, the lids hanging open and the bottoms empty.

'Don't think it was animals,' Uncle Jesse said.

I felt bad for my uncles. The finger graveyard had been theirs, a place away from the whirlwind of my aunts and cousins to commemorate their common bond. Seeing the dirt all torn up by someone for no reason other than to be an asshole angered me.

My uncles picked up their coffins and brushed away the dirt. Uncle Daniels had built them well. The walls remained strong. No burrowing insects had tunnelled their way through underground. The missing fingers must have rested in a state of grace.

A determination took hold of me, focusing my deductive skills. I was going to return my uncles' stolen fingers to them. I already knew exactly who had done this. In the halls at school, I'd heard the thumping of a necklace against a teenage chest. I hadn't realised until now the necklace was made of my Uncles' stolen fingers.

Ricky Castle had invested himself in the idea of the occult.

He'd built a clubhouse down by the closed off canal locks. In grade six, his friends hauled mattresses down there to practise their wrestling moves. First year of high school, they tried inviting girls down there, intending to make men of themselves on those mattresses, only to be sabotaged when their expectations were higher than their experience. Ricky used those failed mattresses to fuel bonfires. For hours, he'd stare into the flames for divination.

I hid behind a tree, watching Ricky pace back and forth. Overhead was blue dusk. Although Ricky could see the tree tops silhouetted against the sky, the trunks melded into a black tangle with the rest of the woods. As long as I kept silent, I'd remain invisible.

Before a crackling fire, Ricky yanked the necklace, breaking the string. I heard the bones thump against the warm ground. At first, I thought Ricky was using them as an I-ching; asking questions and throwing my uncles' fingers to point out answers. No. He had a different ritual in mind.

Aunt Pamela would chastise me for violating Ricky's privacy in the woods, but as far as I was concerned, he'd given up years' worth of privacy each time he flashed his dick in the school halls. He'd done this to every girl I could think of. He snuck up on me once, while I was hunched over my science desk, dissecting a grasshopper, and he tapped his dick against the back of my wrist. I took justified vengeance, throwing a stone from atop a hill that left a mark no new hair would grow over, giving Ricky a quarter-sized bald patch just above his right ear. He also developed a squint, and cruel nicknames followed; Popeye and cyclops. I never called him any of those names myself, but never corrected anyone who did.

The ground in the woods began to thrum. My uncle's fingers began to vibrate, bouncing against the twigs and stones. Ricky stopped pacing and looked in my direction. I held my breath, but he wasn't looking at me. He was watching someone else arrive.

I didn't know she was right behind me until two greasy fingers brushed the back of my neck. She passed me by, gliding silently through the woods. Every branch slithered out of her path as she approached the scattered fingers.

Her sandals were made of animal skulls, and pieces cracked off with each step. Each day she fashioned herself new shoes. I hoped I'd never become a pair, that her heel would never rest in the hollow of my skull, her toes poking out through my empty eye sockets.

The Lanky Skin-and-Bones Lady ambled unbalanced, her centre of weight shifting uncontrollably. Ricky stood straight and relaxed, undisturbed by the appearance of the Lady. Like my cousin and Trudi, he possessed confidence she existed and would show up.

She bent over, using her mouth to pick up one of my uncles' fingers (I think Uncle Louis'). She struck her hand against her chin, breaking her old finger off. It landed on the ground with a thump. The digit hadn't been a proper finger, but a rib bone. Uncle Louis' finger slotted into place. The transplant took root immediately. The Lady made Uncle Louis' finger waggle. The taut skin cracked, but she could use the joints just as fluidly as Uncle Louis had before the finger was lopped off in the press machine.

I strained my neck to get a better look at her. The front of her dress hung open when she bent, and I could see the jumble of mismatched bones making up her rib cage. Hunks of skin and fat dangled from them, not enough to cover her front. Inside she was completely hollow.

She attached the other fingers to her hand, replacing the ersatz digits made from chicken wings and the T-bone from a steak. These new additions pleased her. Finger bones with joints had so much more dexterity than the rigid food scraps she had been relying on.

The offering accepted, the Lanky Lady turned her attention to her benefactor.

My Uncles' fingers, her fingers now, brushed Ricky's cheek. She took hold of his chin, and pulled him close enough to share breath. If she had a nose, they would have touched.

Her hand moved over his face, caressing the skin. I waited for them to kiss, and for Ricky to throw himself on top of the Lanky Lady. He'd lay her on the ashes of the mattresses, finally using them as originally intended.

Her new fingers reached for his right eye, the one half-squinted shut.

Ricky gulped. The boy was nervous. I wasn't accustomed to seeing him vulnerable. Made sense the only place he'd drop his guard would be in the dark of the woods, where he believed no one was watching.

She touched his eye. I heard the squelching sound as she dug deep. Ricky looked to be in terrible pain. She placed her other hand on Ricky's shoulder to keep him steady, before pushing the finger in deeper, rooting around inside his eye. He took a deep breath and let it out slowly, clearly choosing to endure the suffering.

She withdrew her hand slowly, carefully. The tips of her fingers pinched a tiny splinter. It was black, thin as a piece of string. She pulled back, drawing the obstruction from Ricky's eye. When the end finally emerged, there was a faint plunking sound, like a tiny rock dropped into a puddle.

Ricky sneezed, not covering his mouth, blowing a mist of spit and snot onto the Lanky Lady's face. The long splinter must have tickled coming out, perhaps having been long enough to reach his nasal cavity.

He rubbed his eye, and when he pulled his hand away, he no longer squinted. Ricky began looking around; at the trees, at the sky. The sights amazed him. He was seeing the world in a whole new way.

With Ricky's eye function restored, it seemed the interaction was over, and the Lanky Lady began shambling away, pleased with her new fingers.

Ricky called after her. 'Thank you!'

The Lanky Lady stopped, her head tilting to one side as though puzzled by his expression of appreciation. Was this the first time someone had thanked her? She continued moving, disappearing into the darkness.

I quickly followed, eager to retrieve the stolen fingers.

The longer I ran the more I gasped for air. My chest burned, but I wouldn't slow down. The branches beneath my feet cracked loudly. The Lanky Skin-and-Bones Lady glided effortlessly through the woods; I could not catch up. The distance between us was slowly increasing.

I called after her, 'Stop!'

She didn't listen, and the darkness swallowed her completely.

My run slowed to a jog, then a brisk walk. Great white plumes shot out of my mouth as I tried to catch my breath. To my mind, the Lanky Skin-and-Bones Lady was ethereal, like a ghost or a dream, and now she'd faded into the mist like Brigadoon. I felt angry to have lost her.

But she hadn't disappeared. There she was right in front of me, slouched at the base of a tree. Her head lay across one shoulder, and her mouth gaped open, gently snoring. No doubt her long trek through the woods had tired her as much as it had tired me. She was asleep.

I approached quietly, not wanting to wake her. She smelled terrible, all her meat and bones rotting. I expected her entire body to quiver, covered in maggots. I pulled my shirt over my mouth and knelt between her arched legs.

The new bones at the end of her hand belonged to my uncles. It wasn't Ricky's right to give them away. He'd stolen them out of the ground. They belonged buried together.

Gently, I pulled her arm away from her body. It felt heavier than I expected. There were too many bones in her arm. Small, broken pieces, so she'd needed dozens of them, not only to make up the length of her forearm and humerus, but to thread the bones together like bundles of sticks. She had no tendons to hold everything in place.

Flaps of fatty chicken skin slid onto the ground, landing with wet slaps. They grazed my hand, leaving a greasy film. I ignored the disgusting sound, and concentrated on pulling my uncles' fingers from her hand one by one. They were slotted to her pig knuckles tightly. I felt like I was trying to pull a ring off a swollen finger.

With a jerk of my elbow, the third finger popped off. Having used a little too much force I stumbled back onto my ass, and the Lanky Lady's hand fell apart. A dozen bones clattered to the ground. Her eyes opened, staring directly into mine.

'I'm sorry,' I whispered. 'I'm sure you'll get more bones soon. People always have things to wish for.'

Her extended arm fell apart, the bones dropping like a row of dominoes. I tried grabbing hold of her to steady her body,

57

but she continued to collapse in on herself. Her head dropped into her chest, breaking through the ribs. The back part of her broke next, spilling shards of bone and meat onto the ground. Her torso toppled, falling over with a damp thud. Only her legs remained together, but you never would have thought they were legs. More like two posts leftover from a garden that had withered decades earlier.

'I didn't mean for that to happen,' I whimpered to the pile of rotting table scraps that had once been the Lanky Lady. I brushed aside the bones and meat, uncovering her head. I could barely recognise her face. The eyes were dead, no hint of a spirit within.

I waited for something to stir. Eventually, drops of rain fell, spreading the pile of remains further. Eventually, I gave up and headed for home.

In the morning, my uncles gathered behind the press shop. Four new plots had been dug, with four tiny coffins resting beside them, waiting to be refilled and reburied.

I brought the fingers in a smooth handkerchief. Once my uncles had determined which finger belonged to whom, they were placed in their coffins and buried. The plots were deeper this time, ensuring neither scavenging animal or grave robber would disturb them again. I knelt in the dirt to plant a couple of flowers. Behind me, my uncles opened beer cans. Drops of sprayed foam landed on my shoulder. Once guzzled down, my uncles laughed and slapped one another on the back as they returned to the press shop.

Uncle Russell forgot to reimburse me for his coffin. I didn't feel much like asking him.

At night, I dreamed of my uncles' fingers buried under the ground in their little caskets, left to rot, and eventually turn back to dust.

Soon, I was again sharing a bedroom with my cousin Emy. Disaster had once again struck the family house. Black mould grew beneath the floorboards, spreading up through the cracks to infect their lungs. The wood was so rotted, Uncle Louis could rip chunks from the floor with his bare hands. The wood was soft, as though it had been laying in the water for years.

Emy's wet breathing kept me awake. She struggled to draw breath. The infection in her lungs both scratched and tickled, making her cough up hunks of phlegm. They came so often she didn't bother with a handkerchief, but spat onto the floor.

At school, we were all shocked by the return of Trudi. There she was, sitting back at her desk, as though she had never been away.

'Did you pick mushrooms in Vancouver? Did you find adventure?' I asked her, not sure how to explain my own encounter with the Lanky Lady.

Trudi scowled at me. She had nothing exciting to report. Her life away had been just as mundane and stultifying as it had been here. She hated being reminded of that by my questions.

I saw Ricky walking down the halls. I expected his eye to have returned to its squint, the sliver of rock regrown, or replaced.

But no, Ricky looked just as he had the last time I saw him.

He even nodded at me, and smiled, as though we were friends.

Hidden away beneath the ground, my Uncles' fingers were going to waste, like books packed into boxes stored in the basement that would never be read again. Those fingers served a purpose on the Lanky Lady's hand, and I'd forced her to give that away. Even after she'd already given away so much of herself.

From the ground, I took Uncle Louis' index finger, Uncle Russell's pinky, Uncle Jesse's middle finger, and Uncle Dale's ring finger.

Deep in the woods, where I saw her fall apart, I tossed the exhumed fingers onto the ground and waited for her to arrive. I didn't have a wish for her to grant. I only wanted to tell her I was sorry for taking away that which I should have let her keep. I wanted to take her hand for a second time in my life, only instead of pulling fingers away, I would be putting them on.

Shame I hadn't fifth uncle, for four fingers can never reach their full potential without a thumb. The Lanky Skin-and-Bones Lady deserved a thumb.

Squatting on the ground in front of the offering, I squeezed my right hand between my knees. The handkerchief I carried the fingers in was now wrapped tightly to clot the bleeding. Inside the press shop, my blood cooled and hardened on the surface of one of the machines. It was so powerful, and came down so quickly, I didn't feel a thing until well after it was over.

COMING
TO TERMS

Tabitha Carless-Frost

'I'm sorry, you've lost me.'

She is young, little more than nineteen, with a head of dark hair that, though twisted up at the back, strains to break free of the clasp that holds it.

One dark curl has escaped near the back of her ear and hangs suspended, drifting lightly in the breeze from the fan on the shop counter.

I want to reach out to that dark ringlet, take it between my fingers and twist it gently, like the cord of an old-fashioned telephone. For a moment, I allow myself to imagine that you might be waiting at the other end.

I repeat my request, but the shop assistant only looks back blankly. She says something else I struggle to hear and so I simply point, smile encouragingly, and put a pound down in front of me.

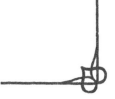

I walk the slanted path through the park, watch the pigeons clutter together under the ash tree, become bored and find a café to sit in instead.

I open my book to read but the words there swim, so I sketch in the margins. My thin ink-threads twirl the letters at the end of each sentence together, knitting them like the dark sprawl of some fungal network. As I deface the page, I am elsewhere – I am motion and blankness and ink bleed on paper. But too soon I am interrupted; a mist of what looks like small, brown snowflakes – which are really rough curls of wood spiralling on the breeze – float down and rest across my page.

I look up. There is a man at the open window next to me, except the window isn't open, it is gone. There is no glass there to reflect the sun opposite, only an opening into the dark inside of the café. The man is bent down fixing, filing, shaving, and buffing the wooden window frame, readying it for the new sheet of glass which rests precariously against the terrace's railings.

I watch him for a long moment, eyes locked on his regular movement. Wood flakes accumulate across my lap. *How had I not noticed?*

The other customers seem unbothered and busy themselves with talk. I wonder if there is some event or gathering nearby that is drawing in so many foreigners because everyone seems to speak something which sounds like German, but a German that is barren of any words I know, any words you taught me. I meet the eyes of a grave little blonde girl who scowls at me before putting her face into her mother's jumper.

I stare down into my lap and look again at the words on the page. Though obscured as they are by the wood-flakes, I can see the black shapes of the typeface clearly. But they are just that: shapes.

Inky scratches without sense.

Ugly spiders swarming on the page, spilling out into the margins.

Senseless, awful scrawls.

I am all hot flush, cold skin; very, very far away from myself and yet horribly close.

I think briefly of shouting out, of calling for an ambulance, for help, for someone. Something in my brain has obviously gone fundamentally wrong, been damaged, is glitching, spasming, haemorrhaging. I imagine a rising tide of blood flooding the soft labyrinth of my mind, drowning the dendrites, bursting each nexus of fragile neural tissue which had, up until now, kept me in place.

I stagger home in a fraught, stumbling near-run. Every street sign, slogan T-shirt, bus title, all read as senseless. Form without content. Shape without meaning.

But worse, far worse, is the sound of talk; snippets of conversation, overheard phone-calls and idle mumblings all push my panic deeper. The noises people make are no longer simply foreign. They are animalistic, bestial. Growls and howls, guttural shrieks, cooing and cawing to one another. My front door is barely open before I collapse into the hallway.

Damage.

All I can think.

Damage.

I am ill. Mad. Broken.

I should go to the hospital, seek help, seek – something. But I can't think of there, can't think what "help" could consist of because more than anything losing language feels like losing you again.

All the words you loved so much, loved so fiercely that it had once made me shamefully jealous, ebb away from me, replaced instead by a steady formless feeling that brings me straight back to those last days on your ward. Reality curdling around us, around me. The blue-toned strip lights and the kind, tired nurses. The papery nightgown you wore and the ever-present sleep around your eyes. The quiet, reedy way you told me to '*sleep, please*' over and over while I sat with you, as I tried to suppress the untameable pointless urgency of it all.

I fell asleep about twenty minutes before you finally went, so, though I don't know for sure, they were probably your last words.

Sleep, please.

I lie on the hallway floor, head on the carpet, eyeline low enough to see filaments of lint, and those words hang in the air like dust, like the sound of a bell that just rings and rings and rings and doesn't stop.

So, I sleep, like I had after the hospital.

64

Sleep for too long; not long enough.

And just like last time, when I wake, I forget for a moment what has happened.

The day is turning to afternoon when I look at my phone.

My finger hovers between the contact icons of my sister, father, and mother. I try (and fail) not to see yours. Each has an image by the name which remains unchanged, yet the letters all look strange – eerily disconnected from their corresponding sounds.

My thumb gravitates towards my mother's icon, but I hesitate, remembering our last conversation. How, in uncharacteristically subdued, almost awkward tones, she had called to see how I was; if I had thought about the funeral; if I was coming to terms with the situation.

I had hung up after a few brief moments.

Coming to terms...

The phrase had felt so clumsily non-specific that I had laughed.

What were the terms I was supposed to be coming to?

Why was I expected to go to them?

What if I wanted to run from terms, to retreat, or hide? Bury them in the garden under thick layers of gritty earth or launch them out into space where the gravitation of greater planetary bodies would draw them ever faster away from me.

Terms, I should have told my mother, are about endings, about the termination of something or the knowledge of its terminal boundaries or limits. I didn't want to be reacquainted with the limits of you, didn't want to draw the boundary solidly and impermeably between us. If coming to terms meant accepting the end of you then I didn't want it.

I think too about our terms of agreement, or the terms I thought we had had: those conditions under which an action might be agreed to be taken. That final action – your terminal act – had certainly broken those.

But there were times too when we had been on bad terms, like when your mother had made me cry in the garden because she said those things about me, about us. How when you had asked me to explain it all I couldn't and instead went blank and quiet.

I had tried *so* hard to speak, but the words just congealed on my tongue. Then your eyes had gone that complicated grey colour – a colour I loved because it was only yours but also hated because it frightened me, because it said plainly you would never really understand me nor I you. It said you had gone somewhere far away, and that I had no way to pull you back.

I stare into the floor.

The cool face of my phone screen rests against my cheek, and I realise that the dial tone's cooing has finally ceased. I can hear my mother's fumbling breath on the other end of the line. But, instead of reassurance, my panic is brought into sharper relief, its edges now serrated, catching on anything and everything in the vicinity.

What if it happens again? What if, when my mother speaks, I hear not intelligible speech or sensible responses but rather only a rasping animalistic something – jumbled near-words in a language I cannot speak, let alone understand.

I hang up before either of us have a chance to utter a thing.

I do not want to know for sure, want instead to leave at least a small, anaemic chance of exception.

I turn my phone on aeroplane mode and retreat upstairs into the darkness of the spare room. It is here that I feel closest to you, in the curled dark of the duvet. Here, you are almost alive again, moving on my screen, moving at my will.

In the days after, I had watched you all the time; in the bath – if I had bathed, at the shops – if I had shopped, while eating – if I had eaten, at my desk, instead of sleeping.

I miss all the little moments I could have glimpsed you without you having known that I could see, when I could see you beyond me, almost beyond yourself.

I watch the same clip again and again, not a video as such but a reanimated photograph, a "live" photo: three seconds of you suspended in time for me to watch and rewatch by holding down the screen. The image is all sunlight and too-small single bed; a backdrop of thin red curtains that brings out a dark warmth not usually present in your skin tone. A cream duvet is around your head, and you are all toothy grin and shining eyes as you mime a frail nun giving a blessing to my laughing torso. For as long as I can hold my finger to the screen, I can delight in this small oasis, dip back into these moments where your resourceful humour is preserved.

I remember the rest of the morning, how when we woke you trilled quietly, a plaintive mewing like a small animal slipping out of sleep. You smelled younger in the morning than you did at any other time of day; soft, pliant, curled like a fern before the dawn has yet opened out its delicate fronds to meet the sun.

You are all quiet-warmth and sleep, dark and nested. Totally yourself.

Your skin – especially the chestnut-shell soft nape of your neck – has something of a hazy, buttery sort of smell: lightly sweet in a smooth, almost-ripe fruit kind of way. Later, at the kitchen table, I will put my face in your neck and you will smell scrubbed, as if the hot water from your shower had ridden your skin of your youness, and you now had to wait a little while before your body was fully your own again.

I watch the looping image over and over for I don't know how long. I try to memorise it, to upload the image and its movements to my mind.

But as I begin to hang tighter to it, something happens.

The morning sunlight within the scene increases to an impossible brightness, filling the room around me with a crushing pressure, and I realise it is bleaching out the details of the image entirely. With rising panic, I see the buffering symbol bloom onto the screen's centre, the glitching tick of it evoking the name the internet christened it with – the wheel of death. The screen flickers for one last time, a pale system-error signal flashing up momentarily before it stops and goes black entirely.

I stare into the screen's blackness, into your absence, into the nothing that has replaced you.

I need to be nowhere.

Away. Outside. Remote. Gone. I want there to be a storm going on, a fierce buffeting of wind and rain which I can run out into, be obliterated by.

But there is no storm, only stillness.

I leave the house.

I drive.

The old ruins are set on heathland, amongst marsh grasses, fenland, mudflats, seawall, salt water, damp soil, damp wood.

I have been there many times before, with you and without.

These are the only times that seem to mean anything anymore.

Last time, we walked the dirt path that wound through the water meadow and up over the spine of the sea wall. I had caught my jacket on the brambles as I jumped the gap between the lull of the dyke and the spit where the ruins sat, and you had fallen to pieces in the bog of the meadow, laughing.

Under the front seat of the car, I find a near-full litre of vodka, a relic of a past-self whose methods of travelling elsewhere were, more often than not, contained within a bottle.

I return to that self, curl up by the ruins' opening and cradle the bottle close to me.

I drink.

I am gone.

But after a while

of being gone,

I start to see and hear things differently.

I lie down–

feel the cool of the earth,

the weight of it below my head pressing up into me.

A marsh bird chirps somewhere

and its trill is like water bubbling.

The rhythm of it shocks me.

Its pattern is linguistic, has intonations.

Their bird-statements, though not senseful, are ambient.

The wind too speaks in sentences that, though unintelligible, possess a very palpable breathwork, something which solicits a feeling words are too small for.

My back grows cold against the dampness of the salt-mud ground.

A thin spear of marsh grass grazes my eyebrow.

Even though it is near-dark now, there is a faint glow outlining the land's silhouette to the west. An ancient burial ground lies that way; bodies packed in below the mud, in line, almost, with my own.

I press my palms flat into cool grit and imagine myself inverted.

Palm to palm.

Dust to dust.

Why hide the dead in the land?

In the dirt?
In the dark?

Why do we have to put you in a hole?

I think of your grave – where it will lie and what will be inscribed on the stone.

What words could possibly do you justice?
As if your loss had not been injustice enough.

I didn't want to hear what they said about you at the funeral.

Didn't want to hear what they didn't say about you, about us.

Funeral eulogies are terminal narratives – they eat up a life, chew it up and spew it back out. They make things simple. Neat. Make things look like they fit and can be tidied away. Their words could only ever be a timid and pale elegy to you, allegorical and bland at best.

I'd rather they just say nothing.

I hate language.

Hate the smallness of it.

Hate the thought of your name on a piece of stone, some phrase plucked from a bible or a www.classicquotes.com webpage and stuck there under it, solid and done – a final reminder of their lack of understanding.

But I don't want to understand anymore either.

Definitions have become eulogies, hollow imitations of the unspeakable delight and pain you brought me.

You opened a door in me. A door between life and death that I am equipped neither to cross nor close – I can only stand on its threshold, wavering between different densities of air.

The breeze on the bank has turned sharp.

A cool salted hush of wind caresses the tops of my shoulders: places where you had once put your mouth to me and left a spray of gooseflesh like a kiss's shadow.

I wander waveringly to the bank, stumbling near the edge of the jetty. I look out at the water, the fading light and the softly bending reeds. I breath slow, deep, feel the salt air make its way into me. I hear the sloshing at the lip of the bank and suddenly I am back with you on that Friday night in May which is really a Saturday morning; drunk and laughing, clumsily peeling off our clothes as the running of hot water steams the bathroom mirror into indiscernibility. Bodies borderless, dissolving and reforming together in the hot water.

To speak then would have been perverse, just as to name that something between us now felt impossible, even sacrilegious.

(I laugh because you had hated God.)

The wind throws ripples across the river and, as it does so, brings the cries of far-off marsh birds to me.

Their coos lament the loss of the light as if the sun might never rise again for them. But I can hear the night-birds are out too. Their calls are ripples in and of themselves, seamlessly mixing water, fading in and out of sense.

I have no desire to set down in words what we were, what, despite your leaving, we are still. Maybe we had never fully understood each other – but we had, at least, never stopped trying to.

Because maybe sometimes senselessness can be pleasurable, like recognising an emotion but having no name for it, or finding surprises in a familiar landscape, or thinking about how much there is still left to know and how much will never be finished.

The evening fades through from dusk's thinness to ink black, and, somewhere in the water below me, a light starts.

A WALKING WOUND

Matthew R. Davis

As the rest of the band ate, Jennifer sat and stared out through the service station window into the night that swallowed up the truck stop beyond. The configuration of the trucks' faces, lit by a lone lean lamppost, made her shutter finger twitch. She was sipping pensively at her iced coffee and framing shots in her mind's eye when Lolly noticed and pinched some of her chips.

'What are you thinking about?'

Jennifer turned to her skinhead drummer with a distracted smile. 'Hmm? Oh, hey, can you hop up? I need to go grab my camera.'

'Sure.' Lolly shifted across the booth's bench seat and stumbled upright; behind the kit she was gracefully brutal, but without sticks in her hands she was a certified klutz. 'Just don't shoot me. I'm a wreck.'

All four members of p83 were showing signs of wear after two straight weeks on the road – thirteen days spent driving in the van and crashing on the loungeroom floors of accommodating promoters, eating meatless junk instead of decent vegan meals, sweating through shows and showering when they could. Much as Jennifer loved Lolly, she was glad the woman was out of smelling distance for a minute.

'Back in a bit,' she said to the others. Careena nodded, munching on a veggie burger that would serve double duty as breakfast, while Bessie was busy drowning her chips in vinegar. Jennifer slid from the booth and made her way across the mop-moistened dining area; WARNING, a yellow A-frame sign declaimed, and the white polished floor was wet with disinfectant like antiseptic on a wound. Glass doors slid apart to allow her out into the night.

She still had the Tarago keys since she'd driven the last shift. She tied her long red hair back and grabbed her Canon and tripod from the footwell before walking across the forecourt, around to the back of the service station where cement gave way to gravel and that single lamppost cast its lonely eye over the truck stop.

Three semis were parked here, their drivers sleeping within or hitting the servo for a shower and a meal – Jennifer thought the middle-aged man she'd seen inside with more hair on his arms than his head was one, the guy sullenly sawing his steak and glancing their way whenever the girls laughed or swore aloud, since his eyes had the same distant road-dulled look as her bandmates. The trucks waited at the edges of the light, dormant giants sat humped in the darkness, their grilles gleaming like fixed smiles. The moon watched the scene from afar, a pale hole punched in the night sky.

Jennifer unfolded the tripod and set up her camera. She adjusted for a long exposure, shuffled across until she had this mise-en-scène framed just the way she wanted it. The shutter counted off three slow shots.

She was about to pack up when a metallic creak drew her attention to the leftmost and nearest truck. Its passenger door was flung open and Jennifer watched as a young woman dropped to the ground, squatting in the gravel for a moment like an animal poised to spring. She didn't seem to notice she was being observed as she rose to her feet and flexed her long fingers, twitched the front of her denim jacket closer together.

Jennifer returned her eye to the viewfinder. The dim woman added another eerie note to the scene: somewhere between mid-teens and mid-twenties, pale face framed by long black tresses, white camisole top under the denim jacket, short black skirt, bare legs down to red slip-ons. She was tall and lean and her arms, her legs, her fingers looked just that little bit too long, a gangly catwalk model fallen on hard times.

The woman walked to the edge of the light and paused, shoulders slumped as if she were exhausted or deeply sated. Jennifer's finger flexed and captured the moment.

She was using a ten-second exposure, and halfway through, the woman's eyes met those of her observer through the viewfinder. The effect was so startling that Jennifer straightened and blinked at the ground until the shutter clacked to announce the time was up. She bent to the fresh shot for examination and saw everything she'd hoped to see – she'd caught a hot one. When she looked up, the woman was gone.

Jennifer frowned. It barely seemed possible that she could have returned to the truck or hidden behind another without being noticed. Little surprise the woman wouldn't want to be seen, though; her presence and appearance intimated a tawdry business she would scarcely want documented by strangers.

Returning her camera to the Tarago, she mused over the woman's circumstances. Since she'd taken to prowling truck stops, they must have been dire indeed – and here was Jennifer, exploiting this desperate stranger's life for art. Some feminist! But at least it *was* art: the woman's eyes had been deep and dark as gun barrels or unlit tunnels, and for all their on-the-road emptiness that Jennifer recognised from the mirror, they'd been electric with some undefinable energy. Black coal burning without flame, negative twin suns.

She couldn't wait to edit the picture.

The service station was a few hours out of Bendigo, their previous tour stop. From there, p83 drove to Geelong, where they arrived late and crashed in the local band booker's back room for the night. Up and out early in the morning, they explored local shops and cafés while Bessie conducted phone interviews with community radio stations. She fielded the usual questions – *what's the story behind that band name?* – before they headed to the venue. After accepting a free pub feed, they loaded in their gear and sat around waiting for the support band to arrive with the amps while Lolly assembled her drum kit. Then they waited while the openers soundchecked, waited for the doors to open, waited for the first band to get on and get off.

Four hours later, they hit the stage and delivered their set with punky elan. The crowd was small but enthusiastic, and

Careena cadged free shots out of the bar staff to celebrate. When midnight had passed and Lolly, the evening's designated driver, had driven the Tarago back to the promoter's house, the women settled down in the back room to relax. Jennifer was finally able to curl up in a corner and upload photos to her laptop.

She smiled at the truck stop pictures, pleased at the way they'd come out, and clicked past them before realising she'd missed that arresting image of the young woman. Navigating back, Jennifer found four pictures almost identical in their composition – including their complete lack of human life.

'What the fuck...?' she muttered. Bessie, changing out of her gig clothes nearby, peered over through the cat eye spectacles that lent her the look of a younger, hotter Shirley Jackson.

'What's the matter?'

'A picture I took at the servo last night... it mustn't have come out. It's not here.'

Bessie yawned and shrugged on her bedtime top. 'There are always more pics, Jen.'

That's not the point, Jennifer wanted to say, but remembered once consoling Bessie after a disastrous performance when her voice had blown out: *there's always the next gig, honey*. She shrugged, wrote the shot off as a missed opportunity... and then remembered checking it in the viewfinder last night, remembered how pleased she'd been to nail the scene. It *had* been captured, so where the hell was it?

Jennifer checked her SD card again, found nothing. Clicking back through the truck stop photos as they shifted in place like a flick-book image, she realised the last of them was different. Fourth time around, the leftmost truck's passenger door was hanging open.

She'd captured that last image after all, but the woman who'd dropped out of the semi like a feral cat was nowhere to be seen. How was that even possible? She hadn't been swallowed by the shadows – there was nothing at all where the woman had been standing, no distortion of the image, and she'd been perfectly visible in the shot Jennifer had seen in the viewfinder.

Enough – midnight was two hours past, her eyes heavy with fatigue. Jennifer closed the laptop, cleaned her teeth, curled up beneath a blanket as Careena turned off the lights. She hoped to fall asleep before Lolly started up with her buzz-saw snore, and tonight, her wish was granted. The drummer let loose a single fart in the darkness, a joke worn thin through repetition, and the next sound any of them heard was Bessie's phone alarm at eight o'clock in the morning.

After a luxurious five-minute shower, Jennifer climbed back into the Tarago for the next drive. Thankfully, it was a short trip to Melbourne and they'd pre-booked a cheap hotel near the venue, so they had a place to chill for the afternoon. While Lolly collected everyone's clothes and did a much-needed laundry run, Jennifer returned to her laptop.

That final truck stop shot remained stubbornly stranger-free. Jennifer chalked it up to a technical fault – had to be that, or else she was already losing her mind like Nanna – and scrolled back further. Here were the p83 girls horsing around backstage at the Bendigo gig. Here was Careena flirting with the cute barman who'd failed to lure her back to his house. Here was the traditional crowd shot Jennifer had taken from the stage near the end of their set—

Her fingers curled into fists and her head darted closer to the screen. Most of the rockers in the half-full room had flocked toward the stage, leaving a few less enthusiastic individuals to hang back by the bar. One of those was a young woman with long black hair and burning, half-seen eyes.

Jennifer zoomed in. Denim jacket, white camisole top, short black skirt, red slip-ons. As if the outfit needed to be verified; those remarkable eyes were proof enough.

It was *her*.

Okay, so: by coincidence, the woman must have hooked a ride from Bendigo the next day and wound up at that service station the same time as p83. While the band was sitting down to feed, she must've been out in that truck paying off her debt to the driver, a thought that made Jennifer queasy. If they'd known how desperate she was, maybe they could have given her a lift. The middle of the back seat was occupied by a box of their seven-inch singles, the rear of the vehicle stuffed with guitars, drums, and merch, but p83 would have happily squeezed in one more woman somehow if her only other option was wrapping her lips around the cock of some sweaty truckie.

But the more Jennifer thought about things, the less sense they made. The crowd had been small enough that she should've recalled seeing the woman there at some point, and this strange synchronicity didn't explain why she'd disappeared from the truck stop photograph. Bewildered, she called out to Careena and Bessie.

'You guys remember this woman?'

They wandered over half-dressed, looked and shook their heads. 'What's so special about her?' Bessie asked.

'Well, nothing. But I thought – I *know* I saw her at a service station night before last, climbing out of a truckie's cab. I snapped her, but look at *this*... there's no one there. I checked that picture after I took it, and I swear she was in it then. It's all just a bit... *weird*, you know?'

'You're fixating on some truck stop hooker now?' Careena pulled a poor-baby face and patted Jennifer's head. 'Either you're learning something about yourself, babe, or it's been way too long since you had a dick in you.'

'Wow, thanks. If you were any more patronising, I'd check to see if *you* had a penis.'

Careena pulled out the front of her knickers and peered inside. 'Nope. But if it helps...'

She picked up an empty water bottle and tucked it between her bare thighs, wiggled it at her bandmates. Bessie laughed and slapped it away. Careena stood with hands on hips, bottle jutting proud, thrusting her plastic phallus in Jennifer's direction.

'Looking for a ride, little girl?'

'Fucking grow up!' Jennifer snapped, seeing only a pot-bellied truckie with his shorts down and a nameless, powerless young woman left with no choice but to allow him into her body. Careena flinched and immediately discarded the bottle.

'Sorry, Jen. All this time hanging around male musos must be taking its toll on me.'

Jennifer forced a smile. 'And here I was thinking you were a feminist.'

'Whoa, whoa. Women are allowed to *think* now?'

Bessie laughed and kicked the offending bottle across the room. 'Take *that*, patriarchy!"

Jennifer turned back to her laptop and stared at the crowd shot, at the gangly young woman whose presence had passed unnoticed. She wasn't drinking or dancing or smiling. She simply stood with her shoulders slumped and her black hair hanging down like some *onryō* from a Japanese horror flick, transfixing the lens with that million-mile stare.

'Enough of you,' she said, and opened the second truck stop image in Photoshop. By the time Lolly returned to dole out freshly washed clothes, the picture was edited and watermarked and ready for posting – but something kept Jennifer from doing so. Maybe she still hoped she could find the fourth photo the way she remembered shooting it, or maybe the scene reminded her too much of that squalid spectre even without her presence. Either way, Instagram went without a post from Jennifer that day. She got ready and followed the girls down to the Tarago, flexing her fingers in anticipation of the upcoming show.

p83 rocked Melbourne's tits off that night, and Jennifer had no cause to think about the strange woman until she picked up her Canon to take her customary crowd shot. She looked around for a denim jacket and long black hair, but while a few rockers met those criteria, none of them were *her*. As she followed Lolly's cue into "Venerate the Generator", the single they were promoting on this tour, she kept her eyes roving through the sweaty mass, picking angrily at her bass as she dared the woman to show herself.

She did not – not then and not after the show as p83 downed free drinks with the support band, and Jennifer told herself Careena was right, she *was* fixating on this one odd detail of the tour, and she flirted with a dude as if her guitarist's jab about lacking action was also true, but when the evening was over she left him disappointed and returned to the hotel with her band, and the gangly stranger only crossed her mind again just before sleep gathered her up and took her down.

Checkout the next morning was followed by a six-hour drive to Canberra, and Jennifer took the first shift, chasing her yawns away with iced coffee. At the midpoint, Bessie commandeered the wheel and Jennifer retired to the back seat with Careena, who had lost herself in a paperback to distract from her mild hangover. With nothing else to demand her attention, her mind backtracked to the disturbing woman in her photographs.

First, she checked her camera to make sure she hadn't captured the stranger in any of last night's pictures. Satisfied she had not, she opened her laptop. The truck stop photos were still devoid of any living presence, though she couldn't shake the thought that the closest semi's dark windscreen was hiding sordid acts from her lens – thick, trembling fingers wrapped in long black hair, wet lips and dead eyes, a selfish satiety. She navigated back to the Bendigo crowd shot and zoomed in to get another look–

And the woman wasn't there.

Jennifer's stomach, near empty, curdled with unease. She'd taken just one shot from the stage in Bendigo, same as everywhere else. There was no chance she'd selected the wrong photograph.

Trying not to panic – *Nanna in the nursing home, looking right at her and demanding to see her granddaughter* – she nudged Careena and tilted the laptop screen her way.

'Remember I asked you about the woman in this picture, the one I saw at the truck stop?'

'Oh, your hooker crush. Yes, Jen.'

'Can you point her out now?'

Careena extended one short-nailed finger to point at the spot where the woman had been standing, then hesitated and let it rove around the screen before giving up. 'I don't know. Look, I'm tired, hon. I need something to eat and a nap.'

'The perils of rock 'n' roll decadence,' Jennifer sighed, but she was relieved. Her friends had seen the strange woman in this image and now they could not, just like her. This was really happening. She was absolutely *not* losing her mind.

She scrolled back through the rest of the tour photos, closely scrutinising each one. The stranger did not appear in any of them. There was bound to be some simple explanation eventually, so she could stop worrying about this now, right? Push it into the folder within her brain where she kept everything that made no sense or no longer bore examination: her ex blandly denying he'd been unfaithful when he *knew* she'd read his sexts; the queasy feeling she'd had around her uncle ever since she'd hopped into his lap at twelve and heard a sharp intake of breath that was more than surprise; the way Nanna looked at her like she was a stranger instead of the beloved granddaughter she'd once spoiled with toffee apples and shiny new two-dollar coins. Slam that folder closed, ignore the way it bulged and strained, and just walk away.

But even though it felt like walking a tightrope over a massive unseen maw, Jennifer opened more folders. Everything she'd snapped this year on her phone or her Canon, everything she'd downloaded from Facebook or Messenger – every p83 gig for which she or others had taken photos – the personal history she'd collated from various sources to keep track of her life these past few years. She skimmed the pictures, looked closer when crowds were present, kept her eyes peeled for a certain face, a certain outfit. And with every minute that passed without finding them, she felt the weight of her bizarre plight easing a little more.

As the Tarago entered the Canberra city limits, Jennifer found herself viewing the first ever p83 photo shoot, three years gone. They'd headed to her local library with a lesbian punk photographer who Careena claimed would lend them street cred and came away with three decent promo shots. They were pretty good, even if Jennifer thought they'd have looked better had she shot them herself.

The best picture caught them standing before a bookshelf, and though it was the plainest of the three, it evoked their personalities so well. Jennifer stood to the left in a thrift-shop flower-print dress, purple tights, and badge-adorned camouflage jacket, her red hair long and wild, an anonymous paperback held against her leg with one finger marking her place at page 83 – the very source of their band name, though the book's identity was top secret. Careena played up her sultry side, one spaghetti strap hanging off her shoulder, the button of her jean shorts suggestively undone, a message written across her knuckles in black marker: NOT4 YOU! Lolly slouched against the bookshelf with arms folded, her distant look, leather jacket, and shaved head giving the impression she'd rather be defying authority and oppression at a rally somewhere. Bessie's mouth gaped open as if she were screaming at the photographer the way she did at a mic, her fists bunched against the front of her Queens of the Stone Age T-shirt like she was about to rip her guts out and let them slop down her tartan skirt and fishnetted legs.

The woman from the truck stop was standing at the end of the bookcase just a few feet from Jennifer, a half-seen slash of wrongness between the shelves and the edge of the shot, one dark eye burning out of the picture like someone was pushing a lit cigarette through it from the other side.

Jennifer jerked back in her seat. She was as familiar with this photograph as any she'd taken herself and would swear on her life it had only ever shown the four of them. She reached out to shake Careena's arm, paused when she saw her friend was serene in sleep. Left alone with this revelation, she stared at the picture as if she expected it to move at any moment – and she *did*, that was the crazy thing, but how could it be crazy if this stranger *was* darting from photograph to photograph?

A thought struck her, and she took a screengrab for future reference. This way, she might have some proof to back her story – and she was going to need it if she reached out to her friends for support.

The other members of p83 knew Jennifer's family history, knew how deeply she feared succumbing to dementia herself. After all, the lyrics to "Peeling Paint", the B-side of their current seven-inch, had been penned by her about just such concerns; even her song "Cannibal Cat Ladies of the Apocalypse", from their first EP, was an exaggerated exploration of decaying sanity. The girls might see any attempt to explain what was going on here as a paranoid assumption of declining mental health – or worse, proof that she'd been right all along and the rot was already setting in. Regardless, the way her sisters looked at her, talked to her, would change. A divide would yawn open between them, and the pity in their eyes would be unbearable.

Like all good punk bands, p83 had some heartfelt points they wanted to get across, and one of those was *believe women's stories.* Now their bassist was petrified of sharing hers with the band in case they didn't. Jennifer could've laughed, perhaps screamed at this hideous irony, but a taut jaw kept her lips locked.

She said nothing to the others as they arrived at a cheap motel near Canberra's CBD, piled their bags into the room, and divvied up the beds – Bessie and Careena got the singles, Jennifer would share the double with Lolly. She slipped into autopilot mode as they ate a cheap chip dinner and headed to the venue to load in. But it would be two hours before the first band took the stage, at least four before p83 could tear into their set, and the wait stretching out before Jennifer seemed intolerable – all that time trying to ignore the elephant in the room, wondering what it was doing behind her back. She told the girls she needed to rest, acquired the Tarago keys, and fled back to the motel.

She opened her laptop and headed straight for the library shot. Jennifer, Careena, Lolly, Bessie, and no one else – the stranger was gone. Expecting this, she let out a sick whimper of a laugh as she pulled up local news. It didn't take long to find the article she was dreading.

Somewhere outside Bendigo, a long-distance trucker had been found dead in his vehicle. No further details were given. Police were pursuing inquiries.

Jennifer's stomach revolted and she bolted to the bathroom. Flushing her half-digested dinner, she explored further folders. Back before p83 she went, flicking through party scenes and university events and her first band's poor attempts at co-opting the identity of their influences.

Eventually Jennifer came to a photo of her at fifteen, taken on a crappy digital camera her mother had bought. She and her former best friend Ollie were posing in her bedroom, all black jeans and bullet belts, emo fringes and eyeliner, as Mum tried to take the shot without shaking with laughter at the sheer *tee-nageness* of it all. The picture brought Ollie bursting back out of the don't-think-about-it folder where she'd consigned him ever since he'd admitted to fingering her while she was passed out drunk in his bed, but that wasn't the worst of it.

Standing in the corner of the bedroom, staring out of the photograph with eyes like deep wounds that never healed, fingers curled into claws: the stranger from the truck stop. The young woman that Jennifer could no longer believe was a woman at all.

'How can you *do* that?' she whimpered, pulling hard on a hank of red hair. 'How can you *be* there?'

She didn't ask the next question aloud, afraid it might somehow inspire her stalker to answer.

And what are you going to do when you get wherever it is you're going?

Jennifer returned to the venue in time to warm up her fingers and voice, faked excitement with her friends as she strapped on her bass, and got through the show like it was any other gig. She took a photo from the stage, even though her trusted camera now felt like a traitor for somehow allowing that haunted creature into her world. She made conversation with punters and signed records and pretended all was as it should be.

She didn't let her guard down until p83 retired to their motel room and she was able to close herself off in the bathroom. Jennifer sobbed softly in the shower, her tears lost in the downpour, miserable with a terror she could neither explain nor outrun. Changing into bed clothes, she slipped into the double alongside Lolly, who was scrolling through her Facebook feed. Noting that Careena and Bessie were already asleep in their beds, she reached for her laptop with a heavy heart and leaden hands.

The stranger no longer stood in the corner of her teenage bedroom, where she and her future abuser smiled and threw shapes like no later taint would ever stain this moment. Jennifer had expected this, and now she roved further back in time.

These photos had been shot on film, the prints scanned and digitised years later. Here was Jennifer pre-teen and pre-emo, before make-up and punk rock and boys; here was the little girl who thought she might one day be an FBI agent like Dana Scully, or perhaps a fashion photographer; here she was at the age of five, her bedroom wallpapered with posters of *Matilda* and *Scooby-Doo* rather than The Used and Rise Against, her red hair in high pigtails and her teeth bared in a playfully ferocious grin.

And here was the stranger, no longer standing in the corner but looming mere feet from the child's back, fingers spidering out toward her unsuspecting host. Her terrible eyes were clearer than Jennifer had ever seen them and still she couldn't make out what lay at the bottom of those cold-coal pits. But what burned out of them was an undeniable *hunger.* The woman was a walking wound that would never close, an appetite that could never be appeased.

She snapped the laptop shut and tossed it onto her bag, hands flying to a trembling mouth. She chewed her fingers in stress, remembered she'd regurgitated her dinner, and her belly rang hollow with want. The room was black now her screen was no longer lit, Lolly having joined Bessie and Careena in slumber, and Jennifer wanted nothing more than to escape into the bliss of oblivion – but she shuddered to think what moves might be made while she slept.

Desperate and terrified, she slid over and cuddled into Lolly's back. The drummer grunted and stirred in the dark.

'You okay?'

'I'm scared,' Jennifer whispered.

'Why?'

She didn't answer, and Lolly didn't push her. She let Jennifer spoon her and held her hand, silently supportive, until she fell asleep. Jennifer thought she might never follow, frightened awake by black eyes burning inside her brain, but she couldn't keep her guard up forever. Somewhere during that dead stretch between midnight and dawn the shadows slipped inside her, and she fell deep into the drowning dark.

Jennifer woke to the feel of warm flesh against hers, the beat of a foreign heart and the song of another's blood ringing in her ears.

The woman – Lolly – was cosy, and she could have stayed there for hours. But she was hungry, ravenous even, and Lolly's warmth only reminded her of appetites that had been suppressed too long. Jennifer pulled gently away and rolled out of bed in the dim, one bare foot falling on the cool lid of her laptop. She silently opened her bag, fetched some clothes, carried them into the motel bathroom. It wouldn't do to wake the others. Too many questions.

She dressed in the cold dark, her eyes and hair colourless in the mirror. When she was ready, she slipped back into the room. Lolly was emitting a thin snore; the others were co-cooned in their beds, faceless, silent.

On her way to the door, Jennifer paused by the splayed square petals of an open cardboard box. She reached in for a "Venerate the Generator" single, flipped it over to see the band shot on the reverse sleeve. There was Lolly, gurning like a comedian; Careena, pouting in a borrowed feather boa; Bessie, winding her long blonde hair around her throat like a noose; and Jennifer, deep unlit-tunnel eyes inscrutable behind curtains of black hair, long-fingered hands plucking at the open front of her denim jacket.

Outside, the predawn darkness lay thick upon the city like chilly tar, hushed and heavily pregnant with the tension of a jungle sensing a predator. The streets were almost empty, but there would be weary taxi drivers, early joggers, shivering indigents; wherever game gathered, there were always strays – the desperate, the lonely, the lost. Her belly ached like an old wound. How long since she had properly fed? She would find something, someone, and soon.

Licking her teeth in anticipation, Jennifer smiled at the shadows and stalked into the dark heart of the city.

MOTH{ER}

Chase Anderson

My first memory was of her room, white and bathed in light. I sat on the floor, trying to help Mother with the laundry, folding towels much larger than me. The walls were clean, the hardwood floor shining. A breeze carrying birdsong filtered through the forest into the open space.

Mother had studied colour science at college, where she met Father. She taught me how hanging glass prisms in the windows made dancing rainbows on the walls. The clear light held all the colours within, she said. It bounced from surfaces to your eyes to show you how something truly looked. I didn't understand, but I liked how all the towels were blue, like the sky, like our eyes.

'You look just like me,' she said, 'when I was your age.' Sometimes she would pull out photos of her brothers and sisters, children lined up on a bench. I'd never met these people. Which face was ours? I pointed to a person and asked if that was her.

'No, dear, this is me.'

I searched her face hard for similarities but found none. The picture was from a really, really long time ago. People changed. Maybe I'd be able to tell when I was older.

I stopped thinking about faces and listened to the soft birdsong instead.

They tried to teach me at preschool, but the teachers weren't as good as Mother. She'd already taught me all about colour and light, so my finger-paints never turned into a brown, muddy mess. Miss Teacher told us that pink was a colour but I blurted out, 'No, it's not, it's a hue.' I was put in time-out because she wouldn't accept I knew more than her.

'Preschool is just to learn how to get along with other kids,' Mother said. 'Or for kids with bad mothers who work all day.' I had a good mother but bad teachers, I told her, so they never taught me how to make friends.

I waited for Mother to tell me how, since she knew so much. She looked down at me from her seat on the bed. There was a white wicker chest between us, which always creaked when I touched it.

'You're supposed to figure that out yourself,' she finally said. 'I can't do everything for you.' She kept talking, and my gaze shifted to the prisms in the window. A coating of dust blocked the light from getting out, or maybe in. There weren't any rainbows on the walls. I walked over to fix that.

'What are you doing?' Mother snapped. 'I'm talking to you,' she huffed. 'Maybe this is why you don't have friends. You don't listen.'

She had to be right. If Mother got frustrated with me, the kids who didn't know me surely did, too. They wouldn't give me a chance if I didn't try harder. I'd show her I was smart, just like her, and could figure things out on my own.

Miss Teacher pulled me aside. I flinched, ready to be scolded again. 'You're going to be a big sister,' she said. But she had been wrong about things before, so maybe she was wrong about this, too. I asked how she knew. She smiled. 'Grown-ups know these things.'

I was unconvinced.

Mother and Father never said anything about it, so I knew Miss Teacher was wrong. A few months later, she mentioned it again.

'I am?' It had been so long, I'd forgotten the previous conversation.

She laughed. Not a real laugh, but the kind people force to pretend to be feeling something else. 'When your mom goes to the hospital to have the baby, we can make her a card to celebrate.'

Mother and Father said nothing when I got home. Miss Teacher was wrong again.

One day Father picked me up. 'Where's Mother?' I asked.

'She's in the hospital. For a little vacation.'

I knew grown-ups said things like that, to mean something else, so kids wouldn't know what they were talking about. They wanted to surprise me with the baby! That was why they'd kept it a secret.

When Mother came home, she went straight to her room and shut the door. I waited in my room, listening for her to come out, to tell me the surprise, but she didn't. I crept to her door and opened it.

She was lying in bed, a big quilt on top of her. It was dusty from hanging on the wall, the bright oranges dulled to yellow, the white expanses greyed and fuzzy.

'Are you sick?' I asked. People went to the hospital or stayed in bed when they were sick.

'It's nothing,' she said. It was dim, with the blinds drawn and the curtains askew. I knew she was lying but I had no idea what was wrong. She didn't look sick, she didn't take any medicine.

The next day at preschool, I asked Miss Teacher if we could make a "get well soon" card. Mother would like that.

Miss Teacher got down to my level and looked me right in the face. 'This isn't something a card can make better,' she said. I really wanted her to be wrong, but something told me this was the one time she was right. It gave me a bad feeling in my stomach, like butterflies trying to escape.

Mother made my lunches and drove me to elementary school. That's what good mothers do, she said. Sometimes she helped me with my spelling. Remembering the order of the letters was hard.

'FRIday ENDS my week with FRIENDS,' she said.

Friday didn't mean that for me. I didn't have friends. But if I said that, I'd be arguing, and then she'd be around me longer, and I didn't want that.

Her hair was short now and she looked lumpy in the sweat-shirts and sweatpants she always wore. There were always big, beige band-aids on the backs of her hands.

Whenever I was around Mother too long, my head would get dizzy and I'd feel like I wasn't really there. I didn't like that feeling, so I tried to stay away from her. But she was my mother, a good mother, so why did being around her feel bad?

I asked a teacher. She got very serious.

'Is your mother hurting you?'

Where had that come from? She never hit me, she never would. I told the teacher that.

'Oh, so you're uncomfortable around me?' Mother asked a few days later. I didn't know how she'd found out.

'No,' I lied, even though it was a really bad one. There was no way I could make up a story to have her think something else. But what else could I say? The real answer would hurt her feelings and make her mad at me.

'Well, that's fine,' she said. 'Sometimes I don't really like being around you.' The corners of her mouth kept moving, even when she ceased to speak. I wanted to run away, but I knew that would make things worse. She left first, going to her room and all the things in it so she wouldn't need to come out, except for dinner.

'Don't upset your mother,' Father told me when he tucked me into bed.

'I won't.' Another lie. So many things I did upset her. Or even things I didn't do. I couldn't trust what I thought I knew. Things always turned out wrong when I did.

In middle school she stopped making me lunch, but she still drove me to school, since that was what good mothers did. I knew that wasn't true, though. The other kids had divorced parents, or only their mother, or they took the bus, and they were always happy around their mothers.

I met their moms: some wore sloppy clothes or had short hair or messy houses or no jobs. Why did those things in my mother make me feel bad?

There was something wrong with me. The kids in the books I read solved their problems by trying hard. I tried and tried, but it never worked.

So I stopped trying at all.

'Can you explain why the sky is blue?' the test question asked.

'Yes, but I don't want to,' I wrote.

'Why did this character feel this way?'

'I don't care.'

'What happened in the year...?'

'Stuff.'

There was something wrong with me, everyone said. They took me out of class, they made me take a bunch of tests for babies. Which shape is a triangle? Which face is smiling? Draw a house, a dog, you, your family. They made me use crayons. I thought about using complementary colours, how I couldn't blend the wax into new hues, but why bother? This was a punishment.

The man running the tests took my paper and looked at it for too long. Somehow, I got it wrong. Maybe I really was stupid and my lying fooled everyone. He asked me who each person was. Me, the shorter one, Father with the black hair, Mother with the yellow hair.

'And what are these?' He pointed to the two lines rising from the top of her head.

They were... I didn't know what to call them. I would see them sometimes, but not always. Obviously, I shouldn't have drawn them. 'I think I coloured too fast,' I said. I couldn't tell if he believed me.

'And what about these?'

I'd drawn big blobs on either side of her stick figure. That sense of being far away came again. I said the first thing that crawled out of my mouth.

'Butterfly wings. I saw a big butterfly outside today.'

'I need you to draw reality,' the man said. 'Not what's in your imagination.'

'Okay.'

He handed me another piece of paper and I drew exactly what he wanted so this would all go away.

'............did you hear me?'

'Could you say it again? The TV is loud.'

A lot of things were making noises: the air conditioner, scraggly animals in cages, the rustling of papers under my feet as I shifted my weight. I didn't want to look at them, but I didn't want to look at Mother, either. Her face had gotten blobbier, fuzzier, her eyes darker. Bandages spread to her fingers, bare at each joint and making her hands look chunky and segmented.

'I said............'

She was saying words, but it was nothing – white noise, swallowed up by the lumpy webs clinging to the walls. Every time I was here, there was that dizziness, that sense of things not being real. Shapes in the corner of my vision squirmed. Father never said anything about it, but then again, he barely went into her room anymore.

'Did you hear me?'

'Yes.' I hoped she wouldn't ask me to repeat it, but I began to try to guess what would be the right answer.

'Good, finally.' She rearranged herself on the mattress. Puffs of dust floated into the air. I turn to leave and rushed out, but in my haste I knocked a box over, objects crashing into each other. Dust and must filled my lungs and I coughed, my eyes watering. How could she stand this?

I scuttled for the door. The hallway was still a mess of cobwebs and cramped space, but at least the walls were still white. I leaned back and stared at the ceiling light, willing my body back under control, through my eyes, not some ghost over my shoulder.

There was a moth in the light, struggling, crawling over its desiccated brethren. How did he even get in there? Did he not see the bodies? I thought to set him free, but I was too short and there was no room for a ladder or even a chair. It's just a moth, I told myself, it can't comprehend the situation it's in. Maybe it'll just fall asleep and never wake up, that's better than being chewed up by some creature.

I knew that things weren't normal. I knew other people's parents left the house, they had people over and knew their children's friends. They let them go out and have fun. I'd tried telling people before about what things were like at home, but no one believed me. I couldn't go out because I'm grounded, everyone's house was messy, I was exaggerating.

Of course no one believed me, I've lied countless times, for little things that didn't matter, for big things. Remember in third grade when I lied to the principal? I always lied about studying. Everyone said that: my classmates, the aides, Mother. I was the accumulation of every mistake I'd ever made, and no one would let me forget it.

But college... that was a fresh start. No one would know me, I'd have a dorm room, it wouldn't come pre-loaded with stuff I wasn't allowed to throw away.

Mother said she'd take me to visit, but she didn't leave her room, not even to eat dinner, so I wasn't disappointed when she didn't. Father took me to a college that specialised in colour science. The campus was open and bathed in the light of the spring sun.

'It snows a lot, though!' the tour guide said. 'It gets cold!'

Insects didn't do well in the cold. That meant they wouldn't be squirming on your clothes or in your books. They wouldn't find their way into your room.

But it was an expensive school and all our money went to Mother, for doctors to fix her hands, for more things to fill her room with, things that got trampled underfoot and chewed full of holes. And that, somehow, was my fault.

All my effort went into studying. After school, I used the small freedoms I had to spin into greater tales of success.

Everyone embellished their college application essays, so it was okay. And it wasn't like anyone would believe the truth.

'Show me the letter.' Her arm reaches out, fingers unfurling in a series of clicks. I can't tell if I'm seeing dirt or tiny hairs. They waggle at me, waiting.

I hand it over. She reads, eyes unmoving. A moth lands on the back of the page and flutters, trying to find a grip. There is no way I should feel it from where I stand, but the microcurrent shakes the hanging threads, worms undulating at the disturbance. I can feel their eyes on me, scolding me for daring to disturb their peace.

'Why didn't you get a full scholarship?' is all she can say.

'They save those for the athletes.' And the really smart kids, I leave unsaid; you can't fib your way to better grades.

'But it's so far away, I won't be able to visit you whenever I want.'

'It's the best school for colour science.' Lying has gotten easier with time, and she no longer bothers to learn about my life. The only things that she cares about stay in that room.

'Aww, you want to be just like me!'

In this room it's difficult to think in words. There's too much movement. Creatures reach for me through the bars of their cages, moths fly by, worms threaten to drop on me. The bulb and the window, both layered in dust, warp the light into a false hue that your brain thinks is orange. But, under all that, it's still white.

A decade and a half ago I sat on that floor. It was clean. The room was full of light. I remember tiny details – the crystal prisms, the rainbows on the wall. Mother was smiling and upright, not hunched over by the weight of her wings. Her hair was long and flowing, not twitching antennae that sensed disturbances in the air. Her hands were soft, warm, with pliable skin and fingerprints. The hands of a human. Of a mother.

How could such wretchedness share the same space as something that had been so pure, so happy? Maybe that was a lie, too, something I had made up to convince myself that I'd once had a Mother and not... this. This thing that grasps me and chews me full of holes and makes my skin crawl. This thing that no one would believe even if I told them.

'Did you hear me?'

'That's right,' I lie. 'I want to be just like you.'

THE DUBLIN AUNTIE

Johanna Zomers

From the passenger seat in the hearse, Gerald O'Neill watched the rain pool on gleaming varnish while his son, Martin, under his slim black Italian umbrella, supervised the graveside. The coffin was a new shade, hinting at the depths of an expensive and exotic wood. He wondered if there'd be a newer and more fashionable hue in vogue by the time he himself was interred in this same cemetery. He'd been feeling increasingly drawn to the imperturbable silence of the expanse of gravestones, finding himself thinking of blessed rest in the midst of hubbub such as his recent ninety-third birthday, full of balloons, neighbours, cake and Guinness.

Birthdays were for show, just like funerals. The cake was from a bakery, the words and roses in hard icing as fake as the expensive veneer over the particle board of the coffin. He thought of the early days, of the days when Siobhán's grandfather and his own joined forces to build raw pine boxes, smelling of the carpenter's shop. He'd prefer that but it won't do for him, for Gerald O'Neill and the fine family funeral parlour he nurtured during his emotional turmoil after Moira returned from Dublin and married the barman.

His own departure will showcase all the respect, deference and dignity that money can buy at O'Neill Funeral Home. His only son, at the helm for twenty years now, will do the right thing. All cynicism aside, Gerald O'Neill, undertaker, has maintained the patina and dignity of a well-loved pillar of the community and he knows he will go out in style.

His will likely be the first date of death engraved on the elaborate granite stone waiting in the storeroom at the monument maker. Siobhán is still in the full of health despite a family history of heart disease. She hasn't had the stress he's endured over the seventy years of running the funeral home. She only had the respectability and eventual affluence and security, while he struggled with accounts and payables and for some time even took on a secret second income, sending cadavers to the medical school in Dublin. That was the greatest stress of all, each illegal trip by night with two body bags in the hearse, while the empty caskets stood locked, ready for burial. The money got him through but it was years before the nightmares about being discovered stopped. You never knew what could surface years later, like the recent terrible scandals of the buried babies in the septic tank in Tuam.

The rain was heavier now and the mourners fled the graveside. Martin will be happy. They can fill in the hole and place the sod and wrap it up, working fast without maintaining the deferential respect needed if the family lingers as they do on warm sunny days. He wonders if Martin has ever resented bearing the burden of inheriting four generations of gentle care of the recently deceased, weighed down with their histories and secrets. Did the unspoken rule that he would follow in the family footsteps weigh as heavily on him as it had on himself decades ago when he was faced with doing the right thing by his own and Siobhán's joint family legacy? He can't recall when it became normal to know the levelling truth that death is where it all ends up – that everything in between is just something to be gotten through before the grand finale, embalmed and commemorated on the carpeted platform at the end of the long-hushed viewing room in O'Neill's funeral parlour.

Professional or not, Gerald expects Martin will feel a lurch in his stomach at the sight of his father's dead body – in recent years he has felt a similar lurch at the funerals of relatives or friends – none of which allowed him to show his true emotions. Today, he feels particularly numb watching the slow lowering of Moira's husband, whom he still thinks of as the barman. A nephew, Moira's only living relative, home from his lawyering career in America, stands impassively, his face shadowed under an umbrella. In the candlelit church, Gerald realised he was craving signs of familiar resemblance, no matter how small.

It's a full October downpour now and the men are working quickly with shovels and a tidying broom. Flower baskets are set in place. The green plastic carpet has been rolled and set into the unmarked truck which has pulled up. The hearse has O'Neill Funeral Services scripted in flowing gold on the rear window, all the better to be recalled by the mourners following the cortege, but the truck is unadorned utilitarian black. It comes out discreetly, bearing the tools of the gravedigger's trade, the wheelbarrows, the fake grass carpets, the small die-sel-powered pump, often needed in areas with a high water table. The deceased didn't order up a watery grave.

Martin shook off his umbrella and set it into the rear of the hearse.

'You could have turned on the heater,' he said to his father. 'Defogged the windows.'

Gerald shrugged into his overcoat. He wished he could go home for tea and a nap and let it all slip into dim memory. Instead, he makes the statement voiced as a question, as he has after every funeral for seventy years, 'We'll go by the reception to say hello?'

The windows are clearing with the heater turned on full and Martin pulls the hearse through the cemetery gates and onto the quiet road. Gerald has always loved that this graveyard is outside of the bustle of town. You can stand on the slight rise near the centre and look out over the fields to the distant glint of the lough and the river. The O'Neill family plot lies on this rise. No water pump will ever be needed in the square of wrought-iron fencing with the tall slender plinth surrounded by smaller crosses and tablets of grey or pink granite. The one waiting at the monument maker for his own name is grey, al-though Siobhán had voiced a desire for the pink.

Warm steamy air, voices, laughter and the hospitable smell of coffee and beer greet him as Martin pulls open the pub door. Two tables of drinkers near the fire look up as they make their way to the back room, where a long table is set with trays of sandwiches and sweets, coffee urns and tea samovars. Martin takes his coat and his own to the row of hangers at the rear. The room is crowded and Gerald looks for the American nephew.

He has the excuse of going there to extend the usual compliments on how well the service went, the eulogy, the final parting at the graveside, heaping praise upon a family wise enough to use their services and not that of the cheaper and more recent Mohan's Funeral Home up the street. He's done it so often by rote. Today he is glad for the familiar words that he hopes will take up the space of the words he wants to ask.

People make way for him, greet him as he slowly crosses the crowded room. O'Neill's is an institution in Brudenell, although there are few enough of the old familiar faces and family names who would care or even remember Siobhán's father, much less the grandfather. Some nights when he has trouble sleeping, Gerald counts the dead, the friends and neighbours he has buried in the past half century. After age seventy they went fast. He's the only one of his friends remaining with a living spouse. His old friend Sean has been a widower for two decades, never seeming to find the skills to make himself more than a sandwich in his gloomy kitchen. Kitchens are the first to suffer when the wife dies, as though the light and the fire of existence have been permanently extinguished. There's a reason why the hearth − and not the marital bed − is the heart of the home. At any rate, that's what Siobhán tells him and has been telling him for all the years of their marriage. If it serves her own purposes for believing that, well bless her soul. Sex might be once a week, but meals are three times a day, four if you count afternoon tea.

He does not like to recollect why his wife came to prefer stirring the cooking pots rather than the faded embers of their marriage bed. He sees all these events spread out over his long lifetime, like a movie projector stuck in slow motion. He sees Moira and her little suitcase boarding that long ago bus for

Dublin. He feels her hand on his, her lips for that quick second behind another bus... this one during the more recent trip to the shrine at Knock. He had missed his opportunity after the kiss to admit to his cowardice on that day the Dublin bus pulled out of Brudenell those decades ago. He could have redeemed himself, clarified the unknown simply by asking.

Siobhán has hoarded that kiss as a weapon all these years – the one view she caught of him and Moira and the quick furtive embrace behind the tour bus. He resents most that it was only his own private secret for the length of the trip home, as the instant they closed their own front door behind them, Siobhán told him in a fury that convex rearview mirrors on buses are placed as they are for a reason. She spit out the words, would listen to none of his feeble protestations of innocence and foolishness, had brought his pillow and a quilt to the spare room – a cold and soulless place – and had not relented even for one moment since that day.

The next year, Moira died unexpectedly of a stroke. Moira was the first body he had turned over to Martin for embalming and preparation. He told himself that it was because he knew Siobhán would never forgive him if he didn't take pains to be at home while that intimate process was occurring. The truth was that he couldn't bear to see Moira's lifeless body, to wonder what had transpired there after he had taken the easy way out. Siobhán had nothing to do with it. His banishment to the guest room after the trip to Knock was complete and irrevocable. He didn't care and that infuriated his wife even more. He'd stopped pretending.

After Moira's funeral, he found himself less able to maintain his professional composure. He had to pull out his handkerchief more frequently during the final blessing, at the prayers at the graveside, even at Sunday Mass when he heard a favourite hymn. Siobhán had taken to playing Clannad on their new stereo and Moya Brennan's haunting voice, singing in Irish, sent him outside to the privacy of the rear garden where Siobhán mocked him for mooning around instead of weeding the potatoes. He had no answer.

Without consulting his wife, he set the pub for sale. In the weeks when buyers wandered through the premises, running their unfamiliar fingers over the worn varnished wood of the bar and the booths in the snug, he found himself thinking constantly about how Moira had gone off so suddenly and silently. He tried to remember if there was anything he had missed in the few sparse details of her trip. After the trip to Knock, his veil of wilful occlusion suddenly lifted and a fit of panic overwhelmed him. What could he have been thinking! Young single women disappeared and then returned. On trips to Dublin, he found himself scanning younger faces.

If he'd done the final death rituals himself – the embalming, the dressing of the body, would he have been able to tell if she had ever given birth? If she'd had an abortion – and here he crossed himself – would that have left evidence? Would she have told him the truth then if he had dared ask her directly? Would she have told the truth after the kiss in Knock? What if he had refused to let her take that bus, instead of, like a feckin eejit, accepting her story about her sick Dublin auntie?

But maybe they hadn't done enough to even make it a possibility? That thought filled him with loss and a bleak loneliness. The nuns would have said yes. They liked to fill the young with terrors of the mobility of sperm; you'd think the little feckers could swim from the pool on her stomach to her Fallopian tubes. But who was to say that a few hadn't gotten a head start, it wasn't the clearest of memories from the instant he felt himself deep inside and instantaneously knew he had to pull out. Immediately. Just one time. Just the one time and then the next and the next. Always careful but likely not careful enough. Would she have told her husband, the barman who he was burying today? Too late to ask him.

He'd relived the memory hundreds of times in his narrow bed after his banishment to the guest room in the failing years of his marriage. He'd always been careful at the pub, with Moira, making sure there weren't any mirrors that inadvertently provided a view into the back room, making sure the blinds and the shutters were closed tight, taking the phone off the hook so he could always say he'd been talking to someone if Siobhán did try to call. He'd had it all organised – the late evenings on the vinyl bench after he'd locked the pub behind the last customer, after he poured them both their drinks and turned off all but the small light above the bar. One drink, two drinks, sitting a little closer each evening, drawing her out with questions, laying his hand on her arm and then briefly on her knee. He was more than a little frightened of what might happen if his wooing was effective. He couldn't say he had ever had to woo Siobhán in the same way. It had been all arranged somehow between them without any real effort on his part. Siobhán had been a sensible girl, careful of her pleated skirts, doling out just enough intimacy at unexpected intervals to keep him guiltily committed. A lab rat pressing a pedal. She had a reward in mind, which was a ring on her finger and their last names joined in gilt script on the plate glass window of their families' funeral home. He felt as if he was on some sort of conveyor belt, propelling him into a future he no longer wanted but was unable to stop both the progress of the steps towards their marriage or of his feelings towards Moira.

He'd watched Moira behind the bar, efficiently polishing glasses, dusting the shelves, straightening the packets of crisps on the rack. She was an indecipherable puzzle, mostly aloof but then unexpectedly he would catch her looking at him. He sensed that she was torn between responding to her instincts and her wary good sense. All that efficiency, the slicing of lemons, the filling of cocktail napkins in their holders. He watched her hands flying over the cash register keys on a busy night, imagining her a few hours later, receptive on the vinyl bench after the pretext of accidental touching or brushing against each other when he moved around behind the bar, bringing in a new keg or reaching for a bottle on the high shelf. At such moments, the noisy room receded and all he could feel was crackling electricity. He hated the new evening barman whose shift overlapped with hers on the busy late afternoons. He watched the two of them behind the bar, moving in unison – pull, pour, bend over, reach up. She seemed oblivious to his presence except for the necessary tasks but, to Gerald, it was a torturous dance of lust which excluded him.

Once or twice when his jealousy reached a peak, he was rude, made nasty comments about how she might want to lose a few pounds before it got too crowded in the tight workspace. She looked stricken and he felt justified and righteous in hurting her feelings. He went home early, leaving her alone to close up on a night when they would normally have had their late drinks. He felt virtuous and devil-may-care as he went up to bed early. Let her wonder why he was distant! Let her feel his disdain for the foolishness of their hour together! He pictured her wiping down the counter and sweeping the floor and sadly letting herself out into the rainy night. Just as suddenly he pictured the barman, perhaps having come back in for a late pint, perhaps never having left, perhaps the two of them sitting over drinks sharing stories of the customers and the shock of it propelled him out of bed abruptly.

Feet into his shoes. Umbrella. Keys.

The pub door was still unlocked. He could see a few customers scattered in the room. No sign of Moira. He'd been so sure he would catch her with the barman that he was unprepared to have her emerge alone from the storeroom. The relief at the ordinary sight of her with an armful of crisp packets, was overwhelming.

'What are you doing back at this hour?' she said. He could see her brighten at the sight of him. His heart pounded in his chest. 'We're a pair of crazy fools', he said, not caring if anyone heard. 'Give last call and we'll close a little early.'

The abrupt escape from his short self-imposed exile was gas to the flame. Hardly had he locked the door, hardly had she dimmed the lights, hardly had they entered the back room, before he had pushed her up against the wall and then down into the vinyl banquette. Hands were everywhere, in her blouse, under his shirt, on her thighs, on her nipples. 'Touch me', he ordered, breathing hard against her mouth and she did... after that, there was no question of not finishing it.

It seemed to anchor something solidly in place between them. He was less jealous of the barman. She was friendlier towards Siobhán. During those short intense moments each night he felt that they stamped an imprint of ownership on skin that only they could read. No one else mattered.

Then abruptly, she withdrew from their conversations, avoiding him, averting her eyes, dodging his hand. 'Is something wrong', he finally asked her, not very forcefully. 'Everything is fine', she said. 'I'm worried about my auntie in Dublin. She's not well.'

'What can you do about it?'

She shrugged.

Within the month, she had given her notice, in writing, avoiding his eyes. On a Tuesday, she had come in carrying a small suitcase, collected her final pay. He offered to walk to the bus with her. 'Not necessary', she said. 'But thank you for offering.'

He thought it sounded sarcastic; then he thought it might have been because she was trying so hard to be casual about the trip. He expected her to write, to send a number, to give him a date when she might return. Half a year went by with no contact before he realised that she had cut him entirely out of her life. In a fog of misery, he got himself officially engaged to Siobhán. Then with no warning, almost a year later, Moira returned from Dublin. She asked for her job back and, overjoyed, he said yes, forgetting his new upcoming marital status. It didn't matter. She moved around him in the pub like a stranger, more efficient than ever with a new brittle cheerfulness and a determination to avoid any sort of personal interaction. She spent more time talking with the barman and in less time than anyone had expected, they announced their engagement. Siobhán too had set a wedding date.

After his wedding, Gerald turned his attention to the funeral home side of the business which had gotten busier and busier. It gave him a good reason to stay away, to let Moira and the barman, now husband, take charge. He need only come in on Monday, take the bag of bills and coins from the safe, deposit it, approve the invoices, initial whatever paperwork needed signing. Whenever he was alone with Moira in the back room, he felt impaled on memory: he took to sending Siobhán to do the banking instead. He busied himself with the business of the dying, of raising his only son Martin, of telling himself that emotions and regrets were of the devil.

A few years later, there was the dedication of the new Shrine at Knock and the entire business section of Brudenell closed their doors for the day and boarded the coach that St. Columba's parish had chartered for the day. It was as festive as the Corpus Christi parade, as jocular as St. Paddy's Day. Siobhán and her mother claimed seats near the front, while Gerald was left to find his own spot on the crowded bus. Shuffling towards the back behind the slow gaggle, he saw Moira sitting alone. No sign of the husband who had likely stayed behind to catch up on pub work. He looked behind him; the bus driver had pulled the door closed. He paused and Moira looked up and then lifted her purse and the raincoat which she had set on the seat. He sat down as the coach started moving.

All around them the laughter and the joking and then the long praying of the Rosary, with which one or the other woman always insisted on ruining every bus or train trip. Hail Mary, Holy Mary... forgive us our trespasses. Moira moved the raincoat over the space between them and her hand stayed underneath the cloth. He breathed into the hum of voices and then he slipped his own hand down to meet hers. It felt only a few moments and, before he knew it, they were at the Shrine. He rejoined Siobhán and her mother until he was able to make his escape back to the other men, to smoke cigarettes and share a bottle behind the bus.

After the dedication, he straggled back to the bus. Moira was the last one out of the basilica. She adjusted the contents of her purse until almost everyone was aboard before she walked around the bus and saw him standing there in the shadow behind the coach. As defiantly as if they were again alone in the back room, she reached up and kissed him.

'I came to the Shrine to ask forgiveness for both of my terrible sins,' she said. 'But I changed my mind about the first. I'm not successful in being sorry after all these years and neither are you. Now we'll both go to hell together.' Before he could respond, she walked away to board the bus and this time she sat down with the woman who ran the fabric store in Brudenell. He climbed aboard, saw Siobhán and her mother in the same seat near the front, noting that Siobhán looked like a thundercloud. He was left to sit with the fabric store husband, who came running back from the pub where he'd been waiting.

In no time at all it seemed, he was home with Siobhán, who unleashed all her suppressed fury.

121

'Convex mirrors on buses are placed as they are for a reason!'

It was the last conversation they were ever to have in the marital bedroom. He felt cheated of everything. Of the heart-stopping rightness of the moment with Moira behind the bus, of the urgency of those early days on the vinyl bench in the back room, even of his quiet domestic boredom with Siobhán. The challenging years of building O'Neill's Funeral Home were long gone. Two thirds of the people in Brudenell had no idea of the efforts that had gone into building the shops and businesses in the town. People chose cremation and an urn ordered from Amazon instead of a gleaming casket and a dignified tombstone overlooking the lough. The new owners of the pub had torn out the snugs and brought in folk singers and disco music and American-style burgers on the menu.

A fearsome desperate delayed grief enveloped him. His emotional cowardice had set their futures in stone.

If any flesh and blood connection existed as a result of what had happened between them, he would never know for certain. In the end, that was the most heartbreaking of all. There was no one now alive who might know the truth that could have changed the entire course of all their lives – the truth of Moira's long ago trip to the Dublin auntie.

PERSONAL SPACE

James Dwyer

It's mostly moving colour. Sands of orange, red, and gold.
Like an hourglass built around me, but with slithers of staring darkness that constantly bleed through. I sometimes feel
there's a creature buried beneath me and every breath it takes
causes the land to heave, spreading my life thin, filling it with
cracks, and causing everything to groan with fear for a sudden shattered end. Until the greed for air is satisfied and that
gulping chest deflates. Then the world returns to where it was.
And I wonder, when my reality becomes so fragile, when it's so
huge and expanded and could fracture at any time, is it better
to love this volatile state? To balance my terror with excitement, and embrace the exhilaration for however long it lives.
Or should I wish things back to how they were before. When
it was calm, and safe, all desperately shielded by the guardians
of memory. Or maybe neither. Refuse to idealise the past, or
search for beauty in the present, all so I can blindly hope for
better in the world that might never come.

The sound of knuckles knocking on wood wakes me from my private frequency. In another world, my hand finds its twin. Fingertips brush along my wrist, touch my device, and turn it off.

I'm back in shared space. In my mother's house. Her bathroom, to be exact. And someone else needs to use it.

I open the door and see that it's my sister's boyfriend. We smile at each other and make small noises that resemble words. Then he walks past, closes the door, and I hear the toilet seat lift. He's not like me, then. Not using the room as an escape to his private frequency, just for its standard function without any complex thought or self-examination.

But then again, sometimes people just need a piss.

I can find it hard returning to an everyday state after leaving my private frequency. Forcing my brain away from grand philosophies and back to basic needs. It can take a few minutes. But, with so many bright colours and loud noises, the outside world soon fills all my empty spaces. Fills it with junk to weigh me down instead of treasures to lift me up.

I look at the device on my wrist with longing, and wonder when I can leave this place again.

The downstairs of the house is chattering with people. Friends and family and friends of family, all here for my mother's big birthday. She's refused to have the number posted anywhere, as if she can somehow hide from it. As if she can multiply the first digit with the zero right there next to it and negate the whole thing.

I see my uncle walking towards me with a beer in each hand.

'One of those for me?' I ask.

'They are in your arse,' he laughs back. 'Your aunt would kill me.'

'Cheers,' I reply, only half-faking my disappointment.

'Coming for a smoke?'

I shake my head. 'I quit.'

'Ah, fair play. I must give them up myself.'

I nod. He lingers. I can see him trying not to ask. Under orders, no doubt, not to say anything about the breakup. After all those years of jokes about when my family could expect a baby or a wedding or an engagement to come out of my long relationship – or for anything of meaning really, to make all those years of love worthwhile.

'Well,' he says finally, 'I'd better head out before she starts wondering where I've gone. Probably think I'm arsing around in my PF.'

I smile at him instead of replying. It's as big a smile as I can manage. Not enough to show some teeth, but any less and people will ask me if I'm okay. And I am. But even if I wasn't, asking me would only ever tip my mood away from it. Getting pushed out by people from anywhere I could happily be, into the places they demand of me instead, battered by their constant self-projections.

Once my uncle is gone, I scan the living room before moving on. A few of my cousins are arguing about something pointless. Shoving their opinions at each other while simultaneously pushing everyone else's away. Unless they miraculously share the same view, in which case they feel suddenly proven right that they are as insightful, smart, and important as they've always believed. But most times people purposefully won't agree, preferring to be the only one who knows what's best.

I see two people staying out of it, blissfully phased away while sitting on the couch, enjoying a free five minutes in their own private frequency, free from the demands of community consensus. If it wasn't for my other cousins, I'd go in there just to be near to my two phased friends. To admire them. A little like watching people sleep, except that their bodies are faded and their eyes are wide open, glowing with gold. Their body becomes a shadow left behind as their sun goes off to explore a different world, but the eyes become truly otherworldly, two blazing lights in the dark. I used to gaze at his forever, whenever he was phased in his PF. He said he did the same to me. But I can never know for sure.

There are people who hate the PF of course, who say that it's just another drug. But there's nothing chemical in the devices. Nothing physical even. It's all purely personal. Like changing channels on a radio, just flicking from one station to the next. For when we all become exhausted from sharing our lives with competing energies and desperately need to be somewhere else. Better than sleep, no matter how vivid the dream. Better than drugs, no matter how ecstatic the high. Better than love... no matter how long it survives before its inevitable demise.

I wander into the kitchen, towards the back garden where I guess my mother will be. Basking in the sun. Swatting away the flies and small talk. Wishing she was alone, while still loving that we're all here. I should probably wish her a happy birthday. Interact in some small way. But I'm intercepted by my sister before I make it. We exchange greetings. Hug. Kiss. Express our love.

'Are we really related to all these people?' she asks.

'I know. It's awful.' We both laugh.

'I wonder how long they'll stay.' She eyes the loiterers nearest us, hoping that they both do and don't hear. She whispers the next bit, 'How long before Mom tells them all to F off!'

'Not long,' I smile back. 'Or we tell them to PF off instead, everyone at once.' I'd been to a party like that. Where everyone was phased out to their private frequencies. An entire nightclub of shades. I only got to see it for a few minutes, before the bouncers asked me to turn on my device too. But it was spectacular. A floor filled with faded phantoms, their blaring eyes a symphony of golden light, all sharing space while in different places. The most wonderful kind of strange.

My sister rolls her eyes. She thinks I spend too much time in my private frequency. Hiding from life instead of being out there living it. But what's the difference? Time ticks by the same either way. And shared space rarely offers peace or happiness. Usually, all it has for sale is fresh anxiety. Always thinking that I should've said something different or done something more, whereas my private frequency only ever brings me joy. Rather than steal my time, it gives me time, to think and feel, to enjoy being myself. Do I use my PF more than most? Maybe. My sister certainly thinks so. But she'll never use a word as sharp as addiction, so instead she uses a thousand smaller jabs. I think of it more as an indulgence. Something I deserve.

'So, how are you doing?' my sister asks.

'Fucking amazing,' I tell her. 'Never been better.'

She snorts at me. 'Right. But, has he text or called or anything since?'

'No. Why would he? And why would I want him to? I broke
up with *him*.'

'I know. And I get it. I do. It's just such a...'

'Such a what? A waste?' A waste of years and love and time
and life and energy that I gave away to someone and can never
get back?

'A shame,' she finishes.

A shame. I know what she means, but still, what a word to
use. Should I feel ashamed to be single? Can I not be one person? Does everyone actually need to be everytwo? Are we all
so small and worthless that we're nothing if not part of something more, even if that more is just a coupling of two people
who can't tell the difference between loneliness and love?

'Listen,' my sister says, 'there's something I need to—'

'I'm sorry,' I say. 'Two seconds.' I touch her arm to soften
the interruption, but I need to get away. 'I'll be right back.'
I flee from my sister, dodging my way through the house,
through the tangle of this birthday, out to the front garden for
some open air. To breathe. To remove the reality choking me,
wrapping tighter and tighter around my neck.

'Change your mind?' my uncle asks. He and my aunt are
seated on the front bench, smoking beside my mom's proud
garden. Wild but lovingly tended, the flowers pop from over-
growth, stretching towards the light. The smoke from my uncle's cigarette wraps around a nearby rose. He shakes the pack
at me.

'No. Thanks,' I reply. 'I just need something from my car.'

I rush away from their temptation, down the garden path, out to where I'm parked. I'm not leaving. I'd never be so dramatic, but I need somewhere private. Just for a minute. Where I can switch on my device, and switch everything else off. I sag into my passenger seat and change the frequency on my life.

Immediately, my breathing calms. Back in the world of edgeless colour, moving around me like smoke now, instead of sand. But the pulse of the world is soothing. No longer the swelling chest of some hidden beast. This is more like a heartbeat: slower, more magnificent, the reassurance of thriving life. The walls of colour are pink and red like roses now, the flowing smoke a sparkle of blue. Flashes of light come with each new beat, glittering the land of my peripheral vision, leaving spots of darkness in my immediate sight. But not really darkness. Just shadows. The ones who always stare at me while I'm here.

Normally I don't move. I don't come to my private frequency to swim around in it. I prefer to remain in place and watch it flow. But these shadows hold me captive now. They've always looked like eyes, a small outside judgement to ensure I remain self-conscious, but today they look like people. Here. In the one place I come to escape. Nothing but meaningless shapes when I look at them from a distance, but as I force myself closer, the shades open up so that I can better see. A blending of energy instead of charges clashing. These people suddenly become the opposite of someone phased. In the shared world, bodies blur and eyes burn golden; here in my private frequency, these shadows have become light, the halo of a person, while their eyes remain black, a darkness my own sight can freely meet.

And I think I know them. All of them my former lovers. None of whom I was with for very long – I've only ever had one relationship that went beyond a year. One that was real. Yet now they all feel meaningful. Pieces of my life, no matter how temporary. But why are they here?

My world of colour beats once more, bringing my mind back to the image of a heart. That I'm inside one right now. Inside my own.

The land and sky closest to me swells once more. I'd always thought of that as breathing, but what if it isn't breath? What if that rise and fall is my heart's constant acquisition of new life and love... More shadows bloom around me at the thought. Old pets. Childhood friends. Everyone I've ever shared an experience with, but more than that, I can see the experiences themselves. As if they too are a person I've encountered, to whom I've spoken, or shaken hands with, or given away one of my dwindling moments. A finite amount of those in my pocket, yet I give a new one away every second, and even more to those I meet. But they're not lost, are they? Because they're here. And they're not wasted. Because these seem more. So maybe, as I give my small pieces to others, they give some of theirs in exchange, each one finding a private place inside me where they can safely stay, all of it becoming–

A fist on glass.

Rap rap rap.

My name being called.

I try to deny it, but the colours around me are already less distinct. My eyes attempt to snatch them back but the act itself only pushes them away. My thoughts are next, less wondrous for being interrupted, their flight cut dead by the gravity of real life. And finally, my feelings, that sense of calm and happiness that everything has meant more to me than I'd admit. Now my joy becomes diluted, mixed with so many other feelings that I can no longer distinguish any one among the crowd.

I turn off my device and see my mother standing outside the car. I roll down the window. I'm not ready to get out.

'Hi, honey,' she says, smiling at me like we're sharing a private joke.

'Hi, Mom,' I reply. 'Happy birthday.'

'For the love of God,' she mutters. 'If one more person fucking says that to me...'

This time my smile is genuine, showing all my teeth. It brings me a little too close to tears.

'Mind if I sit in?' my mother asks. I shrug and unlock the driver-side door. She just looks at me.

'What?'

'Shove over, will ya!'

I look at the driver's seat, at the handbreak and gear stick in my way, and then at the small distance it would take my mother to walk around to the other door.

'For feck's sake...' I make the awkward hop between seats.

'Ah!' she says, collapsing in my chair once I've made room. 'That's better.'

'Too many people?' I ask.

'Too many fucking people,' she agrees. My mom always had a fondness for swearing. Wouldn't say it was an addiction, mind, she just didn't see any reason not to curse.

'So?' she says next. 'Heartbreak any better?'

'Who says my heart is broken...'

My mother places a hand on my leg and gives me a reassuring squeeze.

'No. I'm serious.' I turn to face her. 'Who says that just because we're not together anymore, that our relationship is now broke? I mean, what's the difference between a love I've had for the past ten years, and a love I might have for the next ten? If anything, the love in the past is real, it happened, but the love in the future is imagined, there's nothing there. I really don't see why one should be celebrated and the other mourned.'

I wasn't even sure what made love in the present so great. Was it greed? The safety of knowing there would always be more? Because there was no safety. Never any way to be sure. How can the future shine so bright when it's always shrouded in fog? Or does the present just overwhelm us, always jumping in the way when we try to see beyond it, screaming what it needs until it gets all it wants. All while trampling the past. Smothering it. Burying the old, deeper and deeper until we can no longer remember where to dig. Giving us no other choice but to look for something new that we can bury.

'I know, honey, I know,' my mom says. 'When your father died, I told myself that too. That I'd always have him in my heart. But that's the trouble with memory. It stays still. And we keep moving, bringing us further and further away. But, when you have a love right now... or, in the future–' she smiles at me '–well, it's closer, isn't it. Easier for us to see, so it's easier for us to feel.'

I shake my head, but I don't fight back. I know what she means. Even if I don't know what I mean yet. I felt like I was close to understanding it before, when I was inside my private frequency, exploring the buried darkness of my heart. I even thought I knew what I was looking for. For those ten years of lost love. I needed them to be an unshakeable piece of me. Something real, and solid, that I could still hold and touch, even if it wasn't for very long. But how long does anything need to last? Are we condemned to always need more? Will there ever be a time when we can look at something, satisfied, and smile that yes, it's done.

'Come on, love,' my mother says, giving my leg a slap. 'Your sister and her jockey–'

'Mom!'

'Your sister and her *fella*–'

'He has a name, you know.'

'So? Who the fuck cares about names. Well, they have some big announcement that they want to make, on *my* fucking birthday, mind, and they asked for everyone to be there.'

'Ah no...' There's only so many things that can mean.

'Ah no is right.'

'But that's so stupid. They're too young!' Too young to know herself, or to know anyone else, or to know that this is the right thing for her to do... but should she need to know? Can she not just try and fail and it not be a failure?

My mother shrugs. 'Young and stupid is right, but then, the world would be fairly old and boring without it. Am I wrong?'

'Yes.'

'Ah feck off. Come on, let's let them make their big announcement and we can pretend to be happy for them.'

A fake happiness for a real one. An exchange or an exhortation.

'Okay,' I say. My mom gets out but I stay where I am. She raises her eyebrows. 'I'll be in in a minute,' I tell her. She shakes her head at me, but her frown is soft with sympathy. Easy to confuse with pity, if it wasn't for the love buried deep beneath.

Was that the answer? When we bury something inside us, are we not smothering it but consuming it? Making it a part of us, a small but meaningful piece of our greater selves.

I watch my mom walk back to that house filled with people. I imagine the energy it will cost her to be actively involved. I imagine my younger sister getting married before me, all the life she's planning to live, all the happiness she's hoping to have. All ahead of her. A heart waiting to be filled. But I refuse to think that's better than having one already full.

I switch my device back on.

My private frequency opens up before me like a yawning cave. The ground is a welcoming green, healthy and alive. The walls of my cave are a cloud-scudded blue, looking vast and open, despite being close enough to touch. I don't look behind. Not yet. Instead, I stare in front. To the path dead ahead, a narrow tunnel of rocks and pain, jagged and unappealing, too small for me to fit. To go forwards would mean becoming less than I am now. To cut off pieces of me that no one wants or needs. No one except me. And still I don't look behind.

I don't look back because I can feel him there. His shadow breathing down my neck, the empty gusts of him pushing me forwards when I'd rather just stay still. Other eyes to the side of me gaze out from my private frequency. People I've cared about. Moments that have meant something. Movies that have made me laugh. Books that have made me cry. Music that has fuelled me. Places where I've loved to be. The cynic in me wants to laugh at it, dismissing all this grandeur, because my nostalgia has made everything so distorted. Because not everything in life is beautiful, and there should be enough ugliness here to make this cave wither and rot. Am I to believe that my heart is strong enough to filter out all the malice? To find the strength that comes from weakness, the beauty behind the tears, the light beyond the dark...

I look behind me, and I see that my cave has become a mountain, my mountain an endless range. I see mountaintops blinded by sunlight, and I see the valleys that make my heights look larger still. I see the safe plains of grassland and flowers, with exciting jungles on either side hiding a paradise of lagoons beyond. I see all of it as a whole, even though there's radiance in each piece. And I see them all here. My sister. My mother. The mountains that bring shelter. And yes, I see him too. The grass beneath my feet. The man I wished would be the love of my life. And he is, he was, but just one of them. An indefinite article. A love of my life. The first but not the last, and so important all the same.

I could stay here, I realise. If this is what death is like, an eternity spent in perfect memory, then why not stay? If this is my heart, and my heart is so full, then what's the purpose of my current cave? What reason could I have to go in there, to explore the darkness of that tunnel, when doing so means I must lower myself to a crawl?

But, despite the expanse around me, I can see now that there's no room for me to stay. The irony of a heart filled with love, I suppose; and as I stand here, bursting apart at what I'm seeing, I feel myself inexorably pulled away. To struggle against it would mean keeping my back to the tunnel that waited for me in the dark regardless, my eyes distracted by a fading sight. And it would mean letting those shards and rocks rip me apart as it pleased them, cutting me down as small as they wished, and that wouldn't be me.

So I turn away from the paradise behind me, and give the beauty of my current cave a passing smile. And I charge ahead to the unknown darkness, baring my teeth at every rock I see, ready to smash them all to pieces if I need to, to fight my way out of this crushing moment, and make sure I emerge to a scene where I can more happily be. One as beautiful or imperfect as I choose to create, but wherever I end up, it will be mine alone. My personal space.

COFFEE

Sara Maria Greene

They said our sister Minka was dead.

Dead dead dead dead dead, our mother wept, as she dragged the fringed edges of her scarf over Minka's face. If she were alive, she surely would have sneezed as the fabric tickled her nose, but she just laid there where our father had spread her out on the kitchen table, her skin like the round of hardened white cheese passed around at Sunday dinner, her lips the colour of the frosted cement church steps during midnight mass. *Don't slip. Don't slip*, we'd think and stare at those steps as if it were our eyes, not our feet, that were in control.

Dead, our mother added for good measure and collapsed her head onto Minka's still stomach. We looked past our mother to our grandmother, Babcia. She was hunched over the coffee table, preparing to read the cards. Our ancestors would tell her if Minka was dead. Saint Peter, Saint Paul, Jesus Christ himself, someone would send the symbol – not the Death card.

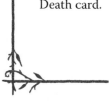

Everyone thinks it's the Death card. We knew she was looking for The Four of Swords. The Four of Swords would mean the most beautiful one of us, the middle sister, the sweet one, was truly gone. Our mother couldn't read the tarot. *Too emotional,* our grandmother said. Our mother was still allowed to go to church with us. No one ever said she spoke to the devil. We didn't want to be like her.

My grandmother's eyes were brown with a gold amber ring around the edges, and sometimes when she looked up from the cards they flickered like candles. She held down the cards with her knotted tuber fingers as if telling them to be quiet while she spoke. *What did they say? The men who brought her here?*

They said she saw a wolf, Babcia. The man who cuts the wood deep in the forest, he brought her into town. He said he found her. He said she had been so scared of the wolf she must have fainted and then froze in the snow. I did not blink.

My grandmother's eyes darkened. She knew what I wasn't saying.

That man was a fucking liar.

Minka would have never been afraid of a wolf. We could see it, my grandmother, my three other sisters, and I. We could see Minka running through the black and crooked pines, the most surefooted, the most steady, but not the fastest of us. We could see the woodcutter press his knee on Minka's chest so he could have both of his hands free. We could see that he forgot just how cold the snow could be until Minka stopped fighting and turned grey. And we could see the lie, puffing from his lips and rising to our stupid brothers like a spindling fog. We didn't always need cards. Sometimes we could split a lie open like we were deboning chickens, deftly pulling out the tiniest sharpest bones, the ones that will kill you if you miss them.

Where are they now? Babcia asked. She meant the wood-cutter and our father and brothers.

They left to find the wolf and kill it, I said.

Lock the door, she said.

She stood up, and I looked at the cards. The Four of Swords was still in the deck.

To my sisters she said, *Take your mother somewhere to cry.* And to me she said, *Mushka, come help.* It was she who nick-named me Mushka, her little fly, little pest. I buzzed around her, learning, learning. I would have drank the sweat from her forehead if it meant I could swallow what she knew. As a baby in the yard, I made the oak leaves my cards, and when I was old enough to speak, I asked for my own deck. My sisters were gifted, but they got bored. They let their thoughts wander. They braided and unbraided each other's hair and talked about boys. They would be good Catholics like my mother.

We will never do this again, Mushka, my grandmother said, but it wasn't true. I would do it again, many, many years later and although by then she would have long crossed over, I would feel her with me, performing the rite. And she had told me that we would never do it again once before – nearly two years prior, when we found the farmer's daughter crum-pled like a sheet knocked from the line by one of our naughty goats. We failed that time, and as we solemnly folded the girl

139

into her funeral shrouds, my grandmother whispered that it was nature, not us, who'd lost her. It was a hot summer full of black flies. No soul would want to come back into a stinking, sweating body. *The other side is icy, Mushka.* I heard her hiss. *You have to trick them a little to pull them back from eternal peace*, then she flipped the girl like the priest flips his black leather bible shut before leaving the pulpit.

When they told me that they found Minka in the snow my mind pulsed with possibility.

Every time my mother screamed *dead!*, inside I whispered, *maybe, maybe, maybe not.*

We kept the caterpillars inside glass terrariums. They were insects that did not know winters because we set their glass in the sunlight, and we watered the green plants around them, and we let them live inside a daydream until the summers, when we set them free as butterflies. There was nothing special about the caterpillar. We would make it special. I selected the black one that looked like it was covered with sharp barbs. The ugliest, the meanest. I knew from prior seasons that when this one transformed, it became a butterfly with red wings, and at each of the four tips there would be a marking like a blue eye. This was what I wanted for my Minka. Four extra blue eyes.

When I brought it to my grandmother, she nodded. It was the one she wanted, too.

Minka looked worse under the harsh kitchen lamps. Someone had crossed her arms over her chest as if she were already in her coffin, and I gently uncrossed them. When I touched her, I heard her laughing in a memory. Her voice was trickling over me like an early spring rain. She was hanging

upside down from her knees in the tree above me and swinging, giggling. *Come on, Mushka, be brave!* she shouted. She
was always doing things like that. "Boy things" my mother
called them. Climbing along the ridge of the roof, riding the
unbroken horses, slopping through the mud with glee. That
was Minka's real curse – to not have been born a boy.

Together, we pried open her slick herring mouth. We
slipped the caterpillar in, and rubbed her throat, feeling it
wiggle down, down. My grandmother said a blessing with her
hands pressed against Minka's face. She said it again. By the
third time, I knew it, too, and recited it with her. Inside Minka,
the caterpillar was dancing on our chant as if it were a song.
It began weaving its silk cocoon around and around Minka's
heart, humming along to the blessing. We said it again and
again until the words began to pull from my mouth like a
strand of thread from a spool and I could not tell where the
blessing ended and where it began. When my knees began to
buckle from exhaustion, my grandmother said, *Now, we wait.*

Three days later, Minka still lay dead on the kitchen table.
If someone tried to shift her body a little bit to set their dinner plate down, my grandmother scolded them. Our mother
returned to weeping and stroking Minka's hair. She stopped
eating, and I watched as her cheeks depressed like footprints
in the snow. Our father and brothers had returned, proud and
content, with a wolf slung over their shoulders. When they
came into the kitchen for meals, they would whisper a prayer
or two over Minka before leaving. But the caterpillar didn't
need their prayers. It had already shredded its floss cocoon
and was preparing to emerge inside the warm black blood of

Minka's heart. I could picture its red wings opening, the way a rose's petals push out from the center of the bud.

Night fell on the third day like a heavy curtain pulled across the sky. I was turned around, lighting a candle, and I missed the moment the butterfly started to pump its wings, pounding inside Minka's heart, beating, beating, dancing to the only song it ever knew. But even with my back turned, I felt my sister's eyes open.

Our mother screamed and began to fall backwards. Our father caught her before she fell. My sisters and brothers stared with their mouths agape. My hands started shaking. Only my grandmother was calm enough to help Minka sit up. *Welcome back, welcome back,* she whispered into Minka's hair as she kissed her.

Minka raised a hand to her own heart, felt it fluttering. Then she laughed. But it was not the dew-drop laughter I remembered. It was a raspy, guttural laugh. A laugh sucked from the bottom of mud. But then she spoke, and it was her voice, and her words were her words, and over time we would get used to the sharpness of the laugh, the way a person could get used to a dog barking in the yard.

Minka was Minka except for the laugh – and the teeth. Her teeth spontaneously chattered and gnashed. She wanted to – needed to – grind them on something. It was like an itch, a horrible itch in her jaw, she said. *A symptom,* our grandmother said, *one of the better ones.* We gave her coffee beans to chew. She ground them and ground them, and it was only then that she found peace with her mouth. It was an expensive habit, and after a few days, we had her spit the grounds in a bucket so we could still use them to make coffee.

She told us what had happened in the woods. My sisters heard a simplified version, but after they went to sleep, I let Minka tell me the true muck of it, the black and rotting spongey bits.

That night I dreamed of picking up a rock and watching black beetles scatter from underneath it. I woke when I thought I heard the rooster cry. I woke when I thought I heard the door hinges squeal. Both times it was Minka sleeping next to me, the sound hissing from her lips. She was the howling wind. She was the mating cicadas. She was the train brakes on rails. She was a stifled gasp, caught in a girl.

Who are you going to believe? the woodcutter said. *I'm a God-fearing man. She's been brought back to life by who? The devil, no doubt. If she were my daughter, I'd do the right thing and kill her again.*

If she were his daughter, she'd be happy to be dead, said my grandmother.

We will leave this matter be, said our father, and oh, how we hated him for it.

They – my parents – would have let her be a shadow, a broom tucked behind an open door, a bowl forgotten in a cupboard. They would have let her silently hover around our lives: my mother, happy to have her back, and my father, happy to have my mother happy. *They want me to be quiet,* Minka told the four of us, as we lay in a circle around her in the yard, making daisy chains. *They said to never speak of it again, but oh how my teeth chatter. They ache: TELL. TELL.* This last part she screamed as she lunged at the sky. The daisies exploded and rained over us, and as the petals cleared from our eyes, we knew what we would do.

My sisters and I, we went out. To every young woman we saw, we smiled, we said:

Come to our house and have coffee. We sat them in a circle, and we let Minka tell them the truth while she gnashed and gnawed the beans, and at the end we brewed them. Hovered over the steaming cups we warned them, and they brought their own warnings like hostess gifts. We drank the coffee laced with Minka's spit and when it was in us, we ran on winged feet, our hearts slamming our ribs. Just try to catch us, just try to hold us down. Good luck. We see you coming and we are already gone, leaving behind nothing but a scattering of footprints in the snow. *Tell the others, tell the rest,* we said.

The story most people remember is wrong, of course. Sometimes they said that she died of fright and was reborn by magic. *She's not going to collapse in a puff of dust or turn into a flock of birds,* my grandmother would angrily scoff when she heard that. Magic is deception. We did the opposite of magic.

They said the woodcutter heard her screams and came running, and not the other way around.

They said that for the rest of her long life, Minka wore the wolf's fur in the lining of her hooded coat. They said that sometimes she would flip it so that the fur side was out, and move so quietly through the woods, you couldn't tell if she was a girl or a predator. But that wasn't true.

The fur made her sad. She never wanted it.

I was the one who wore it.

THE BROTHER LORAX

e rathke

Our friend died just days before turning twenty-five and Lorax spoke at his funeral. Lorax had been his roommate since the first day of college. The funeral was unlike any I'd been to before; though the tragedy of losing a son so young must've torn through his parents, they chose to make his funeral a celebration of his life.

It was beautiful.

When it ended, we who had known him in college went to a Russian restaurant, where we laughed over our moments with him, those gifts of memory which still bloom almost daily all these decades later.

Despite promises to keep in touch, to see each other soon, that was the last time I saw many of those friends until nearly ten years later, when another of our friends died sorrowfully young. Days before he turned thirty-four, we were reunited by his casket and the beautiful words shared to make him rise once more in our lives as if we never forgot him, never stopped spending every weekend hearing his laughter.

Lorax spoke there, too. I hadn't seen him since the previous funeral. He'd gotten fat and bald, arms tattooed up to his rolled-up sleeves. I gave him a hug after the service. We went and got beers at a local brewery, where we made more promises we believed we'd keep.

About a week later, Lorax texted me to meet him at a different brewery, even though it was the middle of the day on a Wednesday. My wife was picking up our older son, F, from daycare. Juggling the newborn, I texted back that I could meet him later, but he responded instantly and urgently.

I shrugged and texted my wife that I was taking baby J with me to meet Lorax.

She told me not to get high.

I always think of Lorax as a college friend, but the truth is that I've known him since I was a kid. We'd been on and off friends for most of our lives, even though we'd sometimes spend months or even years without speaking.

It's been interesting to me, as I live this only life, how often people fall out of my life only to come back and swallow much of it for months at a time. I think of my friend Erik, who almost killed me, and Terra, who I loved so hard and unrequitedly that I nearly killed myself on several different dangerous nights.

Lorax was one of those boomerang friends. He showed me pot for the first time. Lit up my first joint and bowl and blunt. Taught me to pull and hold and not cough. Even sometimes I'd fill in as a dealer for him when we were roommates. He'd text me that so and so was showing up to pick up this much weight for this many dollars. They'd come in and I'd weigh it out and count the money and on they'd go.

He hated those calls. 'Bro, you don't know what it's like to have people hit you up all day for drugs but not one of them wants to chill for a minute.' He snorted, turned to me looking all flavours of sad. 'I'm not a fucking Burger King.'

He said it so earnestly, but I burst out laughing.

Then he snorted again, smiled wide. Laughed too.

'A fucking Burger King,' I said, laughter catching up the words.

He smiled somehow wider and repeated, 'Fucking Burger King, son.'

Carrying baby J on my chest, doing that bouncing, swaying walk all parents learn, I walked towards Lorax, who stood at the bar with his arms wide, waiting to embrace me. Without saying a word, he crossed the brewery to meet me, put his surprisingly muscled arms around me, and hugged me tight without squeezing the baby. He patted me twice on the back, then pulled away.

'Who's this?' He pulled down the Baby Bjorn a bit to see his face.

'This is the wee baby J.'

J had this way of staring at people with his mouth closed and eyes so big and wide that he often reminded me of a turtle without a shell. He gave that look to Lorax but Lorax spoke with him for a full minute before raising his eyes to me.

'Looks like your dad.' He patted me gently on the side of the arm, then led me to the bar, where I ordered an imperial pastry sour that tasted so bizarre I knew instantly I wouldn't finish it. Lorax ordered a Koelsch. We cheersed to our dead friends and then he asked me how my dad was.

147

'Not great. He's got epilepsy now.'

'For real?' Lorax took another sip, then frowned. 'What even is that?'

I tried to explain but barely knew myself. Only knew that it was shrinking his life, killing him, robbing him of so much agency, the way it had robbed his mom of her final years. While I spoke, I kept up the swaying and bouncing. Funny how habitual it becomes, this constant movement to soothe children, to keep them from screaming or interrupting our lives.

We talked about normal things. Politics, art, Godzilla. He told me he'd taken up carpentry, that he was working at a different brewery downtown, that he was selling the mushrooms and pot Dabs had started growing during his PhD.

He kept busy and even though he smiled a lot, laughed at almost everything, I felt there was a strain within him. Right at the corner of his eyes or in the way he fidgeted without something in his hands, the way his hand flexed while he held his glass of beer.

I have a tendency towards projection, however, so I didn't push him towards premonitions. Lorax was an odd guy, but also, strangely, the most well-adjusted of us. His life often seemed a mess – chaotic and fragmented – but he never seemed burdened or weighed down by his life or the choices he made.

He made me feel better about myself is what I mean to say. Like being near him made me more normal.

We ordered another beer. Two IPAs this time. Keeping it safe. I was about to ask him about his kids, of which he had many, when he brought up our friend who had died nearly a decade ago.

'I still miss him, you know?'

I nodded because I missed him too. Told him so.

He sniffed like he was crying though he wasn't. 'You know when you went to Korea after college and I went to California?'

Still swaying and bouncing baby J, I told him I remembered.

'No one ever asks me what I did out there.'

'What did you do?'

He snorted, smiled, sipped his beer. 'I don't know.'

I sipped my beer, not really knowing what to say. Baby J squeaked and squawked in his sleep and I did some shushing out of habit.

'He's talking to you,' Lorax said. He said it without emotion, without the lilt that seemed hardwired into us when we became parents. He took another sip of his beer, set it down, and rubbed his hands. 'It's not that I don't want to talk about it. I do. Partly that's why we're here. It's just...'

'Silence becomes a habit.'

He smiled but only with the left side of his mouth. 'Just so.' He let out a big breath and didn't look at me when he started talking. 'You remember Naoko?'

I did. 'You had a thing for her.'

'Did,' he laughed, sipped his beer and held it with both hands while he stared ahead at the bottles lined behind the bar. 'I left because of her. Felt like she was never going to be who I needed her to be because I couldn't be who she wanted. I left to keep from collapsing. I felt often like I was dying. Like my happiness depended on her. Which is, you know, completely fucked and even pathetic, but it's how I felt. I went to California to escape her and discover who I really was.'

I understood then why me specifically and not another one of our friends or former roommates. Everyone knew why

I had abandoned my life first to live in Ireland and then in South Korea in the years before reunification. They had all met her and came to be friends with her independent of me. They knew how I tortured myself over her and how I couldn't let her go, even though I was ruining my own life and, in turn, making her life a whole lot worse. It wasn't bravery that sent me to the other side of the planet, but cowardice. The shame that comes with understanding your own powerlessness.

For me, it was easier to get certified to teach English as a second language, apply for jobs in a different country, go to Chicago to a consulate to get a work visa, and then fly for twelve hours to land in a place where I knew no one than it was to sit down across from her and talk like an adult.

'My mom got me a job out there at a hotel where I carried bags and shit, which worked out pretty well.' He set down his beer and folded his hands, still not looking at me. 'I got connected with a pusher and dealt right there on my job. But after, like, a month of loneliness where I thought almost daily about coming back, about calling her, I took a bus out of town to this Buddhist Temple. One where silence is a requirement.'

Nothing would have surprised me more than that. Strangely, I had done the same thing in Korea after getting fired. I spent only a week there before my need to speak and be pummeled by noise overpowered my desire to be whole.

'It was kind of weird. I mean, it was great at first. The silence and stillness.' He opened his hands, splayed his fingers, as if the memory was written there in his palm. 'I sometimes still crave it. Have you ever seen *These Fallen Angels*?' He turned to me, finally.

I had but shook my head. 'What's that?'

He shrugged. 'Just a movie. It reminded me of *3-Iron* by Kim Ki-duk.'

'Yeah?'

'You showed me that movie one time when we were stoned.'

I laughed. 'I remember.' He had gotten so anxious from the way Tae-suk sort of danced and floated behind Sun-hwa's husband and carried on his relationship as her lover right there with her husband in the same room, oblivious.

'*These Fallen Angels* is kind of like that, except less awkward and violent. It's quieter and haunting. It reminds me of spiderwebs,' he smiled, laughed a bit at himself. 'Ever seen a spiderweb come partially undone and blown by the wind? It's like that.

'The first thing they had me do is sweep this huge hallway. No one said anything so it was all kind of gestured. It took me a long time and when I was done sweeping, they handed me a mop. That took a long time too. I tried not to resent it. Tried to take it like a lesson.' He shrugged, turned away. 'I tried my best for a week. I did the silent meditations and ate the vegetarian food and never spoke a word to anyone.

'After the first week, this new guy showed up. I think he was younger than me and together we swept and mopped everything. I guess that's the job for new people. Other people were preparing meals and taking care of the gardens. I mean, that's what I wanted and expected. I wanted a return to nature. Wanted to turn back time a few centuries and live without a phone or the internet. Instead, I was inside all the time, doing menial labour that seemed as pointless as it was monotonous.

'Me and this other guy sort of became friends, even though we never said a word to each other for the first week he was there. Even so, having him nearby and working with me kept me going. I felt connected to someone, even if I didn't know him. Felt like someone cared about me. We ate all our meals together, side by side. We worked and meditated and so on, side by side. I think had someone done that for me my first week, I would've been able to make it a whole year. Shit,' he laughed, 'maybe I'd still be there.

'But one day while we were finishing up mopping, he pulled out a pack of cigarettes and raised his eyebrows in a way that felt like an invitation. It's dumb, but when no one speaks you get real into reading body language. Little gestures carry a lot of weight without words. And so I followed him outside and he was gonna light up right there, but I gestured him onwards. We walked away from the temple, past the gardens, and out into the street. It was funny. After two weeks at the temple, you start to feel like it's far away from the real world. But then you get out of the compound and look across the street at a McDonald's and a bus stop and the whole edifice comes crashing down.

'I went there to escape and felt like I had but seeing a four-lane street with traffic lights and fast food showed me I hadn't gone anywhere. I was just burying my head. Still, I probably would've kept quiet and gone back had the other guy not handed me the cigarette and told me his name.'

He took another sip from his beer, this one longer. Then he eyed me and J. 'He's a good sleeper, huh? None of my kids were like that. Always fussing and screaming.'

As if in response, J let out a long, loud fart.

Lorax laughed, 'That's what's up.'

'Wait till you smell it.'

He laughed harder, then harder still once he did smell it. For such a tiny body, J let out the raunchiest farts I've ever experienced. Sometimes it made us worry something was wrong with him because we didn't remember if F was that way when he was a newborn.

Lorax asked me if I wanted another beer and I told him I'd get them. With our new beers, Lorax looked down at his feet again, flexing and loosening his grip on his glass. 'His name was Sam. He was tall and skinny. So skinny that he was always pulling up the pants the Temple provided for us. Ate like a monster. Not that he ate more than anyone else, but he'd be finished with his whole meal while you were barely starting yours. Then he'd sit and stare at your food while you ate it.' He shrugged. 'We talked outside that day while we shared a cigarette and then a second. Later, at night, he came into my bed. We didn't say a word and I didn't move a muscle. Scared, I guess. But it felt so nice to have someone near me. It had been a long time since someone...'

He sighed. 'It became like a ritual within all the other rituals of that place. We broke our silence to talk about who we had been while smoking cigarettes at the side of the street. At night, he crept into my bed and by and by as the weeks went on, we began to comfort one another. It felt,' he stared at his wide-open hand again, trying to find the words to describe himself to himself, to me. Then he shook his head. 'He's been in my dreams lately. I never found him on facebook or twitter or instagram or anything. Sometimes it all feels like a dream. I think I could have stayed there a long time. Maybe forever, if Sam had stayed too.'

I swallowed, now bouncing more aggressively as J wriggled and stirred and woke. Lorax asked for him and I handed him over, felt the tension release from my back. Lorax was good with him. Talking to him, looking him right in the face and connecting with him.

But he woke because he was hungry and shortly after I had to take him home to nurse.

We promised to talk again, to see each other soon, but I didn't see Lorax again in person until yesterday.

By then my sons were dead and my wife had left me because she had to move on from all that death and tragedy. Lorax hadn't been able to make it to the double funeral but he'd sent a nice note, texted, and we even talked for a while about something. I don't remember what. Just remember feeling thankful that I stopped thinking about my dead for an hour while Lorax returned us both to who we had been in college, as children.

I was living in a small, shared apartment at the edge of Lake Superior. I'd always hated the cold but as the Earth warmed and became uninhabitable, I found a comfort in the eternal cold of Lake Superior. She remained defiant to the warming world, using her great volume and surface area to control the northern shores of Minnesota.

I had always dreamt of bringing my sons on a polar cruise to show them the icebergs of the North Pole. I remembered crying with F as a newborn while we watched a nature documentary. The immense loss of the natural world struck me so powerfully. My son would grow up in a dead and dying world. There would be no mountains of ice or lions born outside cages.

The coyotes controlled the North after the death of so many other predators. The wolves died out a decade ago and the deer no longer swarmed in the hundreds of thousands. Instead, there were great packs of coyotes making it dangerous to go out at night or to camp in the vast north wilderness with fewer than five armed adults. Perhaps for that reason, I felt that the cold north of Minnesota was the end of the world that I had grown up with.

Lorax showed up at my door. The shock of seeing him was one thing, but he was so immensely changed by the decade since that day at the brewery. He seemed deflated, like too much skin stretched over too little bone. His cadaverous head was now completely bald and tattooed; at the centre of his forehead was a yin and yang made of two fish. But instead of the koi fish, they were muskies. It made me laugh even before I said what's up or anything.

He smiled and began laughing too. I, too, was changed by the years. Where I had been filling out with the body of a dad, I had become a runner after my wife returned to Tennessee. My body stringy and long, the way I had been in college when we became like brothers to one another.

I let him inside and introduced him to my roommates, who both made excuses and left us alone. They weren't really friends, but they were kind enough and I thanked them later for giving me time with my friend. I suspect they did it partly not to be roped into whatever social interactions would be required of them.

We talked for a while like old times. I never asked him why he was at my house or how he found me and he never explained. Ever since the internet went down, we all just returned to living the way we had in the 1990s. People come and go. Sometimes you could catch people on the phone, but only if they were home. It led us all back into the cities and squares that had disappeared when we made digital interactions the focus of our lives.

He never mentioned his kids, I think, to keep from reminding me of my dead. We avoided talk of cars and alcohol for the same reason. When the sun began to fall, we decided to get dinner and walked to the restaurant down the way. I asked if he had a gun and he laughed because of course he did.

It wasn't until the end of our bean burgers and cauliflower wings that he brought up that day in the brewery. 'Do you remember when I told you about that monastery I went to?'

I did, of course.

'I never got to tell you why I left.' He swallowed and waved away my explanation, the excuses for not getting together again, for letting so much time go by. 'I'm going back. That's why I wanted to meet with you again. I'm going back there and we won't ever see each other again.'

I raised my protests, said of course we would, but he shook his head, cleared his throat. 'Being around you,' he said, 'makes me want a cigarette.'

I laughed and he joined me. 'That stressful?'

'No,' he smiled, twisted his napkin over and over in his hands. 'I told you about Sam. That was hard for me to say.' He raised his eyes to mine for a moment. 'I never found him again, you know.'

I didn't but he knew that.

'I stayed there for six months. I think I would've stayed forever with him. Instead I left and got married for a while.'

'Rachael.'

He snorted. 'Rachael. She was all right.'

'She sucked.'

He laughed. 'Nah, she was a good person. Just the wrong one. Or I was for her. You know how it is. But the reason I left,' he kept knotting his napkin tighter and tighter until it couldn't twist anymore. Then he twisted it the other way until it was flat. Slowly, methodically, he began folding it over and over into squares as he spoke. 'About a week after Sam came to the Temple, he got sick and so I was back to sweeping and mopping alone. It was in the basement, on the second day without him, that I came to an area without light. Like, the lights went out. I went back to the janitor's closet and tried changing the bulbs but it didn't do shit. I just shrugged it off and swept in the dark. I figured I'd do this last bit and then let one of the brothers know that the electricity was out. Probably a blown fuse or whatever. I could've fixed it but I didn't know where the electric box was. But so anyway, I was sweeping. I figured I'd sweep until the end of the hall and then come back and mop.

'Except,' he took a slow breath and wiped his face with the folded up napkin before folding it more. 'Except the end of the hallway never came. I just kept sweeping and sweeping. I don't know for how long, but when I looked back down the hallway from where I came, the light was only a few feet away. This astounded me and I wondered very seriously if I was having an acid flashback. I'd had them before but only when insanely stressed out, you know? I tried to take stock of my thoughts and sensations, but everything seemed normal.

'Then I turned back down the hall. Towards the darkness.' He took a deep breath and pressed his hands flat on the table. The tattoos that had snaked up his arms also spilled down his wrists to cover his hands and fingers. To me, they just looked like black smears on his dark skin.

I waited for him to speak but he just stared at his hands flat on the table. I stared at them too. He breathed quietly but I heard him still. Long, deep breaths.

When finally he spoke, he kept staring at his hands. 'That blackness. It spoke to me. Not in, like, words.' He raised his gaze to me for a moment, to make me understand. Then back to his hands. 'I felt it in my bones and blood. Something older than time. Something darker than black. Something deeper than god. It spoke to me and I felt like a rat in a maze. Like the boundaries of my whole life were predesigned by something that I didn't know or understand. And there I was, trapped. Trapped in a space I didn't understand. Not only geographically but philosophically, psychologically.' He raised his eyes to me, pulled his hands back into his lap. 'I went there to find myself or to understand something about myself or the world. I guess enlightenment, yeah. That's the Buddhist way, right? But what I found in that hallway...'

The waiter came, asked if we were all right. Lorax paid and we walked back to my place. On the way, he picked up his story. 'I was terrified. Just completely shook. But I went back again the next day. Time melted there as I stared into the shadow, as the shadow stared back into me. It reminded me of the worst trips of my life. You know when the drugs turn on you and send your thoughts spiralling inwards?'

I did. Do. Told him so.

He nodded. 'I've always felt that there was an edge of sanity in those moments. Every time, I came back and became me again. Or, a different me than the one before, but like enough that no one but me would know. It's why I've always appreciated even my bad trips. Maybe especially them. I feel I finally learned who I was by almost losing myself in dark nights where my soul felt flayed by dragons existing between me and the otherness surrounding us. I felt that getting close to the edge and coming back down was making me more myself and more human, even.

'Staring into the shadow felt like that. Like I stood on a precipice. The wind howling, beating against me, threatening to push me off one side or the other. The sky cracking open above me and the earth shivering below me, as if all existence swirled around me in a single moment that would define not only my life from that day forwards but also every preceding moment back to the instant I was born. I went again and again. But I feel I began to lose parts of me. Like I couldn't return from that precipice at the void without losing bits of me that I couldn't reclaim. And so I stopped going. Sam got better and we grew closer and closer until he felt like my other half.

'But then I brought him there and showed him the shadow.' He shook his head, kicked at a rock but missed. 'It was the last day I saw him. After, he came to my bed like always, but he left in the morning without saying goodbye. I left a month later.'

We kept walking. The crunch of leaves beneath our feet and the sound of the waves down at the shore. I pulled my coat tighter and he pulled his hood over his head.

I saw eyes flashing in the darkness. One set and then another. Then another and another. I took out my gun, aimed it in the air, and fired off a round.

Lorax had his own weapon pointed at the trees. 'How many?'

'Only one, now.'

Lorax nodded, kept his gun in his hands and we kept walking.

When we got to my porch and his body language told me he wasn't following me inside, I leaned against my door. 'You're going back?'

He nodded looking at his boots, at mine. 'Not coming back.'

Behind him, Lake Superior and the swollen moon and dozens of eyes. I swear I could smell their breath, see the yellow of their fangs. 'You think it'll help?'

He shrugged and met my gaze. His tears stood out in the night like tiny dim stars rolling over his cheeks. 'Have to try.'

I hugged him then. Pulled him into me. I kissed him, told him I'd miss him, but I understood. He squeezed me tight, then tighter, and then gradually slipped away. When he turned to face the night, the dozens of eyes, the moon, and the lake, I told myself I understood what he meant about the precipice of sanity, of knowledge and helplessness, as he walked out into that coyote night.

The coyotes cackled and let out their looping calls and I let him go. Let him go out into that night, into the dark, where I'd never see him again.

Inside, I wrote my ex-wife a long letter. In the morning, I didn't send it.

But I have it now, in my hands.

EDEN

Michael Imossan

— *After Logan February*

Tomorrow I may die or not, depending on the world's temper. Maybe the world will have me sit on my verandah – legs rinsed inside a marsh of freshly mowed green. Maybe the flies will buzz or the bees or the wasps – or a smudge of silence will colour the sunset. Lord, you know I floss my teeth in the morning. You know, during Christmas, I let the chickens off their ropes. Tell my friends they were stolen by night. At the meat market, I buy the birds from their cages, set them free and dance to their flapping – because even flight is a kind of music. Because I know, to be caged, is to have your lights turned off. Lord, you know I write poems that have me naked, dick dangling between line breaks and purple honesty. And sometimes, when the night is cold with loneliness, I ask for a mouthful of a lover's dark breast. Lord, you know I pray for the sick, ask that you heal them. And if you (wont) can't, at least give them enough mouth to laugh through their pain. But today, I am not praying for anything serious. I have learnt, through the wide wound of our wants, that even if you gave us flight, we'd still ask to walk. Lord, I am not asking for tomorrow. I just want to be naked. To go back to the garden, have Eve's supple flesh pressed against mine, our teeth biting gently into the apple until we know sin all over again.

THE WOODWORKER

Sidney Stevens

My father once told me he was afraid of me. He said it only once, but I never forgot. I was young and would gather up things from outside – stones, feathers, sticks, dragonfly wings, insect carcasses, wild animal bones – and construct them into intricate towers scattered throughout our eighty-five forested acres. I've come to think of them as shrines to him, which he finally commanded me to clear away one morning when I was five.

'Stop this foolishness,' he growled. 'You're scaring me.'

In hindsight I doubt it was only irritation that drove him, though that was the message I received. I've come to believe he saw himself in me – some fiery hunger to grab the world's materials and remake them into something new – and he didn't like what was reflected back: a capacity to chase inspiration and inner yearnings and forget everyone and everything else already here. I haven't thought of this in years, and don't want to remember now. But I do. Now that he's dying.

I used to bring snacks to his studio each afternoon – shortbread cookies or tea cakes, that sort of thing, his favourites.

His studio was little more than a weather-beaten cabin sitting above the steep ravine that cut through our land. That was before he built his new studio in the same spot, along with a bigger house, an exhibition gallery and his school for apprentices – all now in various states of disrepair.

I'd run my fingers over his chisels, planes and files, tracing the edges of wood he'd just carved, inhaling the scent of fresh walnut or pine. I adored the fine grains and gnarly protrusions. He never talked to me on those afternoons, but I felt we shared this experience as a single soul. I sensed he felt it too in some subconscious way. At least that's what I chose to believe.

The rest of our life outside the studio – the majority of it – was not the same. He talked to me some in that world – ordering me to pass the bread or shushing me and my brother if we got too loud. Of course, he was this way with everyone, including my mother.

'I'm an artist,' he'd sigh from his seat at the head of the oak table he built himself and carved with fanciful leaf and flower designs that reminded me of hieroglyphics. 'I have clients, responsibilities. I need time to create. How else do you expect to eat?'

All of which was true. He was – is – Orrin Merrick. World famous. I simply chose to focus on the deeper communion I thought we shared in his studio, not this "outside" life. But signs of my folly were always there, if I'd bothered to notice.

When my brother drove himself into a tree in 1972 at age nineteen, my father hung his head – in retrospect I swear it wasn't despair I saw as he glanced up scowling through sandy waves of hair. It was relief. One less burden. One less child lacking his peerless preeminence. I followed his lead and buried memories of my brother as deep as I could.

My mother left after that, unable to find consolation here. My father didn't seem quite so relieved to see her walk away. He followed her to the car like a shadow and asked in a small boy's voice when she'd be back. I was fourteen and remember clearly her ignoring him and begging me, 'Please come!' I certainly shared a more immediate and visceral connection with her than my father, and relied on her for all my emotional needs. But my father begged too, in a different way – begged me to stay.

'Guess I'll find another girl to bring me treats,' he said in that same small-boy voice.

I didn't realise the heartache my staying would cause my mother. But it's all so vivid now – her climbing into the car, face etched with ghastly dread of losing all she had left, of grieving alone.

My father moped around for days afterwards, refusing to go to his studio. Even so, it took little time to find my mother's replacement in Marguerite Simmons.

Looking back, I'm certain he didn't really want me. Didn't want the responsibility of nurturing another human being. Even then I realised I wouldn't get the same attentive love from him that I would from my mother. But I simply couldn't risk him finding another daughter – some usurper – to share his afternoons. I understood his passion for rescuing wood from the forest floor and masterfully transforming it into lasting art. At least I could continue standing near that love, if not directly receive it myself. That's why I chose him.

'You weren't an artistic genius,' he tells me this chilly April morning, as I sit with him in his spartan upstairs bedroom, where he's slept since my mother left. His voice is weak, and he looks emaciated lying in his narrow bed. 'I wished for it... You have no idea.'

He seems sincerely regretful that I wasn't a chip off the old block. I want to protest his insincerity, slap him. But this is what he's told himself and buffed into polished belief. There's no way to untangle all my feelings – shame for falling short and disappointing him, the father I love. Rage that he would say this out loud without regard for how it might hurt me. A wisp of hope and stab of defiance that maybe he's wrong. All I know is I'm here. After all he did and didn't do, I've come back one last time to nurse him through death. That's what you do for love.

'Rest now,' I say and pull up the thin white blanket he's used for years. He's nothing but bones now. I swear I can see them through his skin. And he smells like old cheese. His face is all gaunt angles and sunken features, misshapen like something a child might mold from Play-Doh. Incredibly, he still has that mop of waves, completely white now but every bit as full. I can't wait to escape his room.

'I helped you all I could.' His voice is hardly a whisper, holding me near a while longer. 'You never made a success of things... I couldn't keep funding you.'

He means my failed acting dreams and divorces (two of them).

'There was that small part on Broadway,' he says, 'Then nothing else.'

'I had big roles with Tannery Run.'

He sighs and looks away. 'Community theater.' His blue eyes, faded and cloudy, stare at the trees outside.

He's right, of course. I never achieved anything like him – the great Orrin Merrick. Pulled himself up from nothing and coiled his name around the planet. Don't I know? He became the greatest woodworker of his generation. Took woodworking into the realm of the sublime. After acting I became a real estate agent (moderately successful), and before that I was a department store clerk. Everyone wanted his sculptures, a table, a desk, a door, a mantelpiece. They still do. His works are in museums and mansions around the world. I'm merely his dutiful but unremarkable daughter. Don't I know?

'At least I tried,' I say. I should pat him or offer some comfort. He is, after all, dying. But I can't. In that way I'm a chip off the old block.

He nods and closes his eyes. 'You tried...'

He believes I don't know where the wrong turns were. It's true I don't dwell on how my life didn't play out right, how I drove it down an abandoned road. But I know exactly where the unfortunate junctures lie, where forward momentum went awry. I just thought I'd eventually point myself in the right direction.

'Do you need anything before I go downstairs?'

He doesn't answer.

There's so much I could say but don't. He failed in marriage, too. There were lean years in my childhood when my brother and I sat in hand-me-downs in the school cafeteria without enough money for lunch. He struggled to make ends meet like I did, often resorting to pruning trees for other people and doing odd jobs. Success came slowly. There were failures.

I remember all this, but he doesn't. Or won't. He never could see the fault lines in himself, the earthquakes he caused for others. Instead he cast his flaws onto everyone else, never feeling them as his own. He could flourish unscathed as long as someone else played "loser."

If only I could pummel him now and shove him towards reality. But he's shrivelled and helpless, and I'm tired. I was on the receiving end of his projections too many times, a crash-test dummy enduring trauma and mutilation in accident after accident so he didn't have to. I came back to him anyway. That's what you do for love.

Here's another unbidden memory – I was fourteen, not long after losing my brother and mother, hovering beside my father in his new studio.

He handed me a piece of wood from his storage cellar: walnut. It was about a foot long with a bulbous burl on top that twisted down to a slim middle and widened again at the other end.

'Use whatever tools you like,' he told me from the doorway. 'I'll come back in an hour to see what you've made.'

Of course it was a test, but I felt new worlds open in me. That wood in my hand was alive. It vibrated so I could barely hold it, as though it was talking to me without words, guiding me to sculpt and burnish it until its soul shone through. He trusted me with it.

It was quiet in the studio except for a gentle rain outside plunking on the metal roof, everything grey and dripping. But I was so beautifully lost it all seemed far away.

I followed the lines and curves of the wood with my father's gouge chisel, scooping out depressions, rounding off edges and shaving off bumps, floating in a heavenly place I'd watched him reach but had never been to myself. I was hooked.

It seemed only minutes before my father returned. 'What's this?' he asked, moving closer.

'A goblet,' I said, handing it to him. It had sprung from the inherent shape and grain of the wood. The cup on top tilted slightly, like a flower towards the sun, but not so much it couldn't hold liquid. The stem spiraled down and around like a vine, swirling to a broad bottom base. It wasn't finished. It still needed sanding and staining and polishing, but I could already see its completed beauty. I was proud of my work.

He turned it around and around in his large hands, my lovely goblet bending and curving like the body of a dancer. He held it at arm's length with a frown as though it was something from alien space, and finally set it down. His eyes widened briefly as he studied me, and in that moment I swear I saw something like fear. The same fear he spoke out loud when I was five.

'The work of a child,' he muttered and looked away. 'This wood was clearly to be fashioned into the arm of a chair or door handle. My mistake in thinking you'd see it as I do.'

Fear drained from his eyes, dismissing me. He pointed towards the door. 'You tried, and that's to be commended... Now run along.'

I remember slinking back to the house, shoving past Marguerite baking in the tight kitchen, and retreating upstairs to my room with hot shame burning my skin. Banished from the only place my father and I could connect. Little did I know I was dismissed forever. Never invited back to his studio, merely because my goblet wasn't what he would make. For once proclaimed inferior, he and I and the rest of the world believed I was talentless. The great man had spoken.

I linger in his doorway this morning. The spring days are getting longer and warmer as the weeks drag on, but I can't seem to shake the chill hanging around me. Odd how shame, once remembered, is still as fresh as it was fifty years ago when he exiled me. He can barely move his head now. His breathing is shallow and his eyes are closed most of the time. He eats so little. It won't be long. He wants me by his side more and more.

I've longed my whole life for him to need me like this. And yet I can't stand to breathe the same air now or touch even a bit of him, especially his old decrepit hands that have had the luxury of creation all these years.

I've never let myself hold another piece of wood since that day in his studio. The thought actually pounds like a migraine in my brain. I want to forget what I never got to have.

Marguerite called a few months ago to say my father was "failing." Her word. It shouldn't have surprised me. He is, after all, ninety-three. Even so, I didn't expect it so soon. The bigger surprise, though, was that Marguerite, twenty-two years his junior, was also failing. She didn't mention it then. Colon cancer. The same kind that took my mother ten years after she left.

'He wants you here,' Marguerite said softly. 'Can you come for a while?'

I almost said no. I hadn't spoken to them in five years. They'd just quietly slipped from my life. Yet I quit my real estate job and took on nursing them both. I can't explain it – some combination of being needed – loved – again, wanting to escape the humdrum-ness of my life, and the urgency and regret I believe I heard in her voice. These are my reasons for being here.

'He's sorry,' Marguerite told me a few days before she passed. She was beautiful to the end, lying on the brocade sofa in the sitting room, long hair spread out on cushions, nearly white but still full, like when my father first brought her into our lives. Her mahogany eyes were just as brilliant too, like glass beads. I sat in a nearby chair, unable to look away.

'Sorry for what?'

'For everything, I think.'

'Everything?'

'For not being a better father.' She paused and held out her hand, which I didn't take. 'You needed compassion and love, not just money. And encouragement. I failed you too.'

It was true, but I didn't say so.

She reached for a canvas bag on the floor. 'I found this in his studio. He told me about it then.'

I peered inside, stunned for an instant, as if my brain couldn't recognise what my eyes saw. There was my goblet. Exactly the same.

'I kept it for you.'

'Why? ...I thought he threw it out.'

'Because it's beautiful.'

My eyes stung with old shame. 'He doesn't agree.'

'He's wrong more than he knows.'

If only she'd said that back then. If only he would now.

'I had a dream after that.' It slipped out before I could stop myself. Useless dream. I'd never told anyone.

'About what?'

'It's silly.'

'Tell me.'

I looked around, desperate to divert her attention. But she lay waiting.

'There was a beast with horns and iridescent scales, bluish-green.' It sounded ridiculous. 'A dragon mixed with something like an elk.'

Marguerite smiled and closed her eyes. 'Go on.'

'A woman in a matching iridescent gown with a cape rode on its back. She wasn't young or old, sort of ageless. She was intimidating and never said a word – but I sensed they were there for me.'

'Remember that dream,' Marguerite said softly. 'Watch it come back someday.'

My father opens his eyes now, staring at me as if my childish dream has suddenly appeared to him. Ridiculous dream.

'All this will be yours,' he whispers. I lean close, barely able to hear him. 'Protect my legacy – I know you will.'

I will. That's my role. It always was. I sacrificed my mother for this privilege. Failed to grieve my brother with her, failed to love her. I assumed our love was solid, robust. Not like the frangible love I had with my father, so much of it hidden. I couldn't risk losing even a twig of that. I believed she'd forgive me, but she died before she could.

Only saps remember dreams, right? Yet he expects me to carry on his dream – the one he made come true. I sacrificed everything to protect it and keep him close. Dumped the courage to hear my own dreams. And yet here I still am.

There's fear in my father's eyes on his last evening alive. Immediately I'm struck with an odd thought: What if it isn't fear of death staring at me, as you'd assume, but the same fear he declared when I was five, as he ordered me to tear down my creations. Or the fear in his eyes when I was fourteen and dared to create what I saw in the wood without him. What if he's still afraid now – no, terrified – that I might have talent, too. Talent he squashed to keep himself elevated, or to keep me in service to him, or any number of other reasons he'll now take to his grave. Did he know what he was doing then? Is he afraid now for his place in eternity?

If so, he doesn't snatch his last chance to say so. And later, after they've carted away his body in a zippered black bag and I've put clean sheets on his empty bed, I creep through the dark house. My house. Empty now too except, of course, for me and his wooden art that fills every damn cranny. Wooden walls lined with carvings. Chairs and tables sculpted from tree trunks, whimsical bannisters fashioned from winding boughs, and desks with secret, odd-shaped drawers – all of them wrung from his mind and hands. I was also wrung from him. We're cut from the same trunk. But he wanted to be king. Utterly unique. I got in the way.

I run my hands over his things. My things now. I'm not gentle. I dig my nails along walls, furniture, whatever I can find, scratching lines into finely carved angles and undulations. Priceless objects by a master artist.

It's criminal, but after a lifetime – my lifetime – of silent screaming at his disregard for who I am, it feels beautiful to etch my fury into all that's left of him.

I wander up to my bedroom closet and pull out the goblet Marguerite gave me months ago. I haven't looked at it since. He was right. It's immature, the work of a fourteen-year-old. I can see what he saw then, but there's also beauty. Its swirling shape in my hands still pleases me. My body almost curls in unison. I can imagine it finished, the lines sanded smooth and the grain rubbed to glowing life with oil and a soft cloth. Years of loving use would have darkened and ripened its finish to satin.

These two perceptions – his and mine – hang side by side like they're on an old-fashioned balance scale. But his tray hangs lower. It still holds more weight.

'He doesn't deserve you,' my father told me once after I left Cameron, my first husband, a fellow community-theatre actor who was sleeping with anyone he could grab. I was so laser-focused on the prince I imagined him to be I stupidly overlooked his indifference until it was too obvious to ignore, right there in front of me on the futon in our cramped apartment. Just one of my innumerable wrong turns.

'You were right to leave,' my father said. I still remember him seated in his favourite leather chair in the study. It's the only time he ever admitted I was right about anything, and I could tell from the grim line of his lips he was sincere. You'd have thought he'd taken me in his arms, brushed back my hair and told me I was his princess and everything would work out fine. That he'd love me forever, and I'd find another man who would love me just as much. That's how completely his words sated me.

Well, I didn't find someone to love. I found Rick Weltman instead, a banker, who said he loved me (I believe he did) but left after two years because I couldn't stay faithful. Yet another wrong turn. Pining for something else. Something more. Another fairy-tale love that looked better because it sat at a distance, out of reach, within my comfort zone shaped by my father.

I assumed I'd never feel as low as I did after those abandonments. But as I clutch my goblet now – my father newly gone – I feel lower. This is a new order of abandonment.

I walk out the front door, past my father's studio to the edge of the ravine, goblet still in hand. I don't feel him around. Strange that some sliver of him wouldn't stay at least for a while. He loved this place. Fiercely. I've always believed he loved me too; just found it hard to show. I've run on that fuel, loving him back with everything in me. You can't explain how a heart in love can forgive anything, accept any behaviour, overlook every truth. It loves what it loves without asking why.

But I've come to the end of fantasy, finally forced to admit what a fool I am. His love never manifested into anything tangible, even one small stick that I could carry with me. The ghastly truth is this: He didn't love anyone. Not in the right ways. Not fully or deeply enough to matter. It simply wasn't in him. I spent my life holding out an offering, but he lived and left without it, never offering me one thing in return.

How do I mend this knothole inside, stuffed with love that never found a place to land? Love he couldn't receive, but also love I never gave my mother or anyone else, including myself. I was so focused on winning him I ended up withholding it all. Just like him. This is grief.

I fling my goblet into the cool, black ravine. A loud cracking breaks the night as it hits trees and rocks, perhaps splintering into a hundred pieces that scatter in the mud below.

'It really is lovely here,' Joan says as we wander towards the studio on a cloudless autumn morning months later. 'A work of art in itself.'

I've asked her here as my realtor, but also as a friend. 'Whatever helps it sell,' I say.

'Oh, it'll sell, even in this shape.'

A sense of lightness moves through me. Relief. I laugh. I need the money. But also there's a sense of loss that surprises me. My father would be heartbroken. I shouldn't care.

We make our way down to the ravine on the woodland path he walked most days.

'Are you sure about this?' Joan asks.

'I am.'

I'm not really. After months of thinking, I still don't know what I want, but I'm tired of mulling it through my mind. I need action.

Joan stumbles on something protruding from the fallen leaves, but catches herself. She bends to retrieve it. 'My god,' she says. 'Is this his?'

I look away. I might cry. My goblet is intact.

There's no explaining how it survived and why it's appeared now. Surely a crazy coincidence. Yet some part of me believes it was meant to happen. It sounds ridiculous. I'd never say it out loud. But that's how it feels in this moment, deep inside me. 'It's mine,' I mutter.

'Wait, you made this?'

I nod. 'I was a kid... I wish he'd taught me more.'

'I don't think he needed to.' Joan traces a finger along the sinuous stem. 'You have to finish this and make more.'

It's the nicest thing anyone has ever said. I want to cover my ears, hold in the words forever. I blink back tears.

'Open the studio again,' she urges.

'No one wants my stuff.'

'They will... turn this place into a museum. They'll come.'

'Oh my god.' It's overwhelming. The risks. All that needs fixing. Buildings to be repaired, fingernail marks to sand away, treasures to be restored. Courage – I simply don't have enough.

'Imagine the headlines,' Joan says, looking around. 'Naomi Merrick carries on her father's work.'

In my dark bed I clutch the goblet like a teddy bear. I try to sleep, but I'm wholly awake. I want to believe Joan, but also I don't. At the heart of things, bottom line, my father's voice is still the strongest of all. I simply can't fail again.

I examine my goblet in the moonlight. For an instant, I flash to the beast from so many years ago. I'm not dreaming exactly. I'm awake. But it's like my mind is playing a game of make-believe. One I have no power to stop. I'm invited to ride the beast. I hate make-believe. I don't want to play. Only saps remember dreams, right?

'Why her?' people whisper as I stand trembling before the creature. 'She's not queenly like the one before.'

I glance from side to side, seeking a place to flee, but assistants arrive to dress me in the woman's dazzling gown and cape. 'I can't wear these!' I try to squirm away. 'I'm not like her!'

They hoist me onto the beast, massive and muscular beneath me. I long to disappear, but can only slouch low. I'm not worthy.

Why not you? This thought comes to me as I move through the crowd atop the beast. *You can grow into her and ride as she does.* That's the next thought. No, wait. *She's something you are already.* I am her. I didn't know.

Love fills my goblet as I raise it to the moon. There's a place, after all, for my love. I don't have to hold it in. Alone. This land, the tools, the wood – they can all hold my love. There's so much here yet to create. There's joy to sculpt and forgiveness, too. Still time to love – even if he couldn't. Time to accept what life has brought me – all of it – and embrace the whole of me, the knots and chop marks but also my special grain and lustre. In this way I can't fail.

ENCORE

Jesse Krenzel

I often wake too exhausted after the dream to go to work in the morning, but today I feel a little better. No tangled sheets twisted taut around me or soaked with nightmare sweat this time.

My tiny cottage is cold this October morning, the pitted wooden floor rough beneath my pale feet as I pull on my green janitor's uniform. I heat a cup of yesterday's coffee in the microwave while I shave and smooth my thinning grey hair. My reflection looks gaunt and worn, but I'm still reasonably fit for a 64-year-old.

The sky is still a grey shroud above Franklin High School when I arrive. The air smells of autumn, with fallen grape leaves wet and rotting in the vineyard across the country road from the high school. The school staff parking lot is empty but for a lonely silver sedan. I park my old brown Ford pickup in its usual place and climb out carefully to avoid twisting my trick back. Two more years to my pension, if I can hold out. After that, who knows.

As I start toward the Admin Building, a woman climbs out of the sedan. She's my age, or maybe a little younger, professionally dressed, probably from the District Office. That's never good. Her skin looks waxen in the cool light, her blonde hair dull and brittle, her eyes tired.

'Good morning,' I say.

'Hello, Albert.'

I don't know her, but she has striking pale blue eyes.

'I'm Joanne Stafford. Joanne Hurley, back in high school.' The image of a laughing blonde cheerleader comes to mind, a classmate from my own time here at Franklin.

'Joanne? Sure.' I smile but dread the impending reminiscence that always ends badly. 'What are you doing here? I thought you moved to Arizona or someplace.'

'Boulder, Colorado. I came back to help my daughter and her husband after the accident.'

'Oh.' I nod as if that somehow explains her appearance in the school parking lot at 6:45 am.

'I was hoping to have a word with you.'

'Really? About what?' I try hard to hold my smile. 'When I saw your car, I thought there might be trouble inside. You know, a broken pipe, vandalism or something.' I thrust my hands into my jacket pockets and try to stop babbling. In her shy smile I see a little more of the young girl in Joanne.

'The trouble is all mine, Albert. I know this is weird, lying in wait like this, but Marty Helms said it was the best way to reach you.'

'Marty? Haven't seen him in a while.' I omit the fact that I actively avoid my former bandmate.

'I need a favour. It's a big ask, but it's for my granddaughter.' She draws a breath to gather herself. 'Do you know about Cindy Stafford? She's a senior here.'

Now I put it all together. 'The car accident. I'm sorry. I didn't make the connection.'

She nods and looks away, holding back tears. It's another high-school tragedy: a kid, a car, and a coma. For two weeks the kid's classmates have been washing cars and selling baked goods to help the family with the medical bills.

'She's a good kid,' I say. 'Is she doing better?' I already know the answer and hate myself for the cowardice of feigning ignorance.

'About the same. It could be weeks before she wakes, or longer. Albert, the hospital is going to transfer her to Los Angeles unless we can raise a lot of money to keep her here. Diane and Doug can't afford to leave their business, but the doctors say Cindy needs family around her.'

I nod. 'Seems like it always comes down to money, doesn't it? Well, I can help some.'

'Oh, I'm not here for a donation. I spoke with Marty about playing a fundraiser for Cindy.'

'Yeah, he could do that. He still has a band, and he's always looking for gigs.'

When she pauses, I realise why she's here.

'I was hoping for a Blue Tones reunion,' she says.

The asphalt at my feet feels like it's turned to quicksand. Joanne's voice recedes to a barely audible distant echo.

'I thought maybe you and Marty—'

'I don't do that anymore, Joanne. I'm sorry.'

'But if you could just–'

'I doubt that anyone even remembers the group anymore.' But even as I say it, I know I've lost. Modest royalty checks still find their way to my mailbox for plays of The Blue Tones' one hit single.

Joanne's face lights up with that old cheerleader verve again. 'Oh, but they *do* remember. Classic rock stations still play "Best Ever". I hear it all the time. People know that song, Albert, and I know they'd come see the original Blue Tones perform it again.'

I fight back the dread that rises around me like a flood. I manage to say, 'I'd like to help. I really would, but–'

'Please don't say no yet. Just think about it for a day or two.' Then something changes in her expression. 'You were so talented, Albert; a number one song while you were still in high school. All these years I thought I'd see you on TV one day, singing something from a platinum comeback record.' She tries to smile. 'We all thought you'd return to your music. But you never did.' She touches my arm. 'Maybe performing again would be good for you too.'

I pull away from her. *Who is this woman to sneak out of my past to manipulate me like this?*

Her eyes open wide. Startled, she extends her open palms as she would to a menacing dog. 'I'm sorry. I didn't mean to–'

'No, I'm sorry,' I say, embarrassed now by my anger.

'I shouldn't have surprised you like this. You're still hurting after all these years. It's just that… I don't know what else to do.'

I stand there mute, wanting only for the conversation to end.

She shrugs and forces a smile. 'Well, that's my pitch, Albert. It's all I've got.'

I nod. 'I need to get to work now, Joanne, but it's good seeing you again. I hope it works out for you and the family.' I start toward the Admin Building.

She calls after me, 'Please think it over, okay?' She's standing there, thin and fragile, shivering in the icy breeze.

'I'll do that,' I say and turn away again.

I trudge through empty school corridors to the storage room that doubles as my office, a windowless, oversized closet that stinks of bleach and floor cleaners. I drop onto a wooden stool and take a few deep relaxing breaths. Decades old music plays in my head, the songs of my meditation. After a few minutes, I open my eyes and begin sorting the day's work orders. By the time I open the door again, the corridors have come alive with staff and students. I walk among them like a ghost, invisible and inconsequential as always.

The rest of the grey day passes like all the others, with anonymous student faces floating past me like dry leaves in a mountain stream. Marty Helms is waiting in the parking lot after work, leaning against my pickup with a hand-rolled cigarette smouldering in the corner of his mouth. My former bass player has thinned with age, a lanky biker now with a grey ponytail, leather vest, and a chrome chain that loops from his belt to the wallet crammed into his greasy jeans.

I greet him with a raised middle finger. 'Scratch the finish with that chain, and you'll have to repaint the whole thing.'

'How're you gonna know?' Marty grins with small teeth yellowed by coffee and tobacco.

'Not surprised to see you,' I say, dropping the tailgate and tossing a discarded wood pallet into the bed for kindling.

'Joanne Stafford talked to you about the benefit concert for her granddaughter?'

'I said no.'

'Hey, the kid's in a coma from a crash, man. Come on. Let's play the old songs for them.' He gestures on a ghost guitar.

'The Blue Tones are done.'

'Not if we're still breathing. Come on, Albert. Why not?'

'You know why not.'

'That accident was a long time ago, man. It was a bad thing that happened to good people. That's life. But now we can do something nice for that family.' I hate the way Marty is using my guilt to get the band reunion he's wanted for years.

'We can't bring back the Blue Tones,' I say. 'You know that.'

'*You* were the Blue Tones, Albert, not me, and sure as hell not Nina or Jacob.'

I slam the tailgate closed. 'Is that supposed to make me feel better?'

'All I'm saying is that you could do something nice for that family if you wanted.'

'What's with this fucking guilt everybody's laying on me today? Don't you think I've got enough yet?'

'You've got nothing to feel guilty about, Albert.'

'Yeah? Well, you didn't kill Nina.'

'Neither did you.'

'Take a look at my rap sheet, asshole.' I push past him and climb into the pickup.

He follows me to the door. 'It was an accident, man. It wasn't your fault.'

I start the engine, desperate to flee the old argument. My intoxication that night wasn't the only cause, but I know that Nina would have survived if I'd been sober.

'Come on Albert, it could have happened to anybody. It was kids in a car.'

I start the engine and back out of the space. When I stop to change gears, Marty is scowling at my window. 'You haven't changed a bit, Albert. Still the martyr. You love that shit, don't you? Love it so much you throw away your whole fuckin' life over—'

The squeal of my tyres covers his words.

I arrive home exhausted and drop onto the bed. The monotonous beige walls are bare but for a single blaze of colour: the framed record album cover of *Introducing the Blue Tones*. It bears a 1968 photo of our band posing among grape vines. It's my altar to Nina. Her light brown hair glows in the golden sunlight, while Jacob and Marty and I crowd around her with our psychedelic print shirts open to our belts. Foolish kids with no idea what life is.

That night, the dream comes again. I smell Nina's flowery scent at the start before she slips from the shadows and floats towards me through a shaft of moonlight. The curves of her naked body are smooth and white as sculpted marble. Her cool fingertips reach out and trace gentle lines across my sweating face. She draws back the blanket and settles astride me. I want to reach out and hold her, to stop what comes next, but my arms are dead at my sides. She leans down, her face inches from mine, and whispers, *Albert.* Suddenly, her body pitches hard to the left and she begins twisting back and forth. Her arms rise, flailing white in the moonlight like a pair of dying swans as she struggles. Then she shrieks in pain. *Help me, Albert! Help me!*

I'm paralyzed beneath her, choking in the cloud of acrid smoke that rises around us, stinking of gasoline and burning rubber and Nina's burning hair. Suddenly, her agony ends in one final grotesque spasm.

And then she's still, a blackened mannequin atop me.

Bitter flakes of charred skin drift down when she opens her seared eyelids. She lowers her peeling face to mine and whispers, *Albert.*

And then I wake.

I lie there in the darkness for a long time with the old Blue Tones songs flowing through my head, thinking about the night that Nina died in my burning car while I lay broken a few yards away; and I think of the decades since then, alone, with no wife, no family, my only legacy an old hit song and a lifetime of avoidance; and I think about Marty, a pathetic old rocker still chasing the glory days of his youth, and about Joanne Stafford, whose comatose granddaughter she prays might still live a useful life.

In the morning, I call Marty.

Marty's band, the Blue Dudes, is his Blue Tones tribute band. They rehearse in a detached garage behind his brother's home on the north side. They've tacked old carpet to the inside walls to quiet the sound, giving the place an odour of damp mould and stale cigarette smoke. They play the old Blue Tones songs and a few covers twice a month over at Oak's Bar and Grill.

Marty introduces me to the band. I've met his 17-year-old niece, Diane, and heard her versions of Nina's vocal parts. She nods towards me and resumes texting from a bar stool in the corner.

Brothers Devo and Nick Hartz perform parts played by me and Jacob, the original drummer who died of an overdose decades ago. The Hartzs are in their 30s and work at Marty's Chopper Shop. The brothers exchange a look when they see me. Devo reluctantly extends a hand and nods. His head is shaved to show off an intricate black Maori tattoo across the back of his neck.

Nick shakes my hand and sweeps his long black hair back over his shoulders, saying, 'I thought Marty was joking about you going back on stage. You think you're up for this?'

'I'll give it a try, asshole.'

The rehearsal starts loose and sloppy but tightens up after a few minutes. By the end, we've covered a third of the Blue Tones' original songs. When the rest of the band has left, Marty lights a cigarette and squints at me through the smoke. 'Whaddya think?'

'We won't embarrass ourselves too much.'

'How about some of your new stuff?'

'Who says I've been writing?'

He plucks a piece of tobacco from his tongue. 'Hey, this is me you're talking to. I remember the day Nina came to practice, all excited about a song you played for her over at your little love nest. I don't think the world would've ever heard "Best Ever" if she hadn't sung it for us right then.'

His memory is weak in details, but I get the message. 'I wrote it for her. It was supposed to be private.'

'But see where it took us?'

Looking around the mouldy garage, I laugh out loud for the first time in months.

That night, I lay in the darkness, waiting for the dream to come. I begin to tremble with the first whiff of Nina's scent. Then, instead of her usual ghostly appearance, I hear her singing a soft melody in the distance, a melody that I pray I'll remember.

With each rehearsal, I find myself thinking more about Nina, remembering her toothy smile, the little snort she made when she laughed, the feathery touch of her curls on my face, and always her scent. One night, I hear her voice in the next aisle at the grocery store, smooth as warm cream, speaking on her cell phone. I cruise the store for ten minutes looking for the source of the voice but can't find her. At school the next day, I get a whiff of Nina's perfume and wander through the corridors sniffing the air like a hunting dog for twenty minutes. My heart skips a beat when I see a girl in a flowing white dress like Nina's at the end of a long hall. I start toward her before I realise it's just a student.

News of the Blue Tones reunion spreads through the town and up the peninsula. *The Times* runs a two-column story about the benefit concert, dwelling on the irony that the band was ended by a tragedy so similar to that of Cindy Stafford's. Tickets sell out so quickly that Joanne discards plans for folding chairs and makes room for another 200 people. It will be bleacher seating and standing room only on the gym floor.

Traffic is gridlocked for a half-mile around the school on the night of the concert. I park in the staff lot and slip into the gym through a back door. The rest of the band is waiting behind the closed stage curtains, excited and nervous. Marty is visibly relieved when he sees me.

'Man, I had this terrible thought that you changed your mind.'

I only smile. No point in admitting that I briefly considered it in a selfish moment.

Marty has dressed for the occasion, trading his dirty jeans and leather vest for khakis and a blue and black Hawaiian shirt. We didn't discuss clothing, but my own brown and green Hawaiian shirt gives us the vague look of a mismatched uniform.

Joanne appears backstage, clutching a piece of wrinkled notepaper. She offers a teary smile as I strap on my old Stratocaster. The murmur of the unseen audience behind the curtains is charged with excitement. We tune to Devo's keyboard. When I tell Joanne we're ready, she touches my arm, says a soft *thank you,* and slips through the curtains with a microphone in hand. The crowd greets her with a generous applause. She thanks everyone for coming, says a few words about Cindy, and finishes with our introduction.

'We are so honoured and grateful to have Albert and Marty and their band with us tonight to play songs that they haven't performed together in a very long time. Please join me in welcoming the Blue Tones!'

The curtains open to a burst of cheers and applause as the audience gets its first look at the Blue Tones in almost 50 years. The applause wanes far too quickly, and I suddenly see myself and Marty as the audience does, an old school janitor and a motorcycle mechanic in goofy shirts on a high school stage. My limbs lock, and my hands turn to stone.

Marty starts the walking bass line from "Good Days Past," the B side of our hit. My heartbeat falls in with the bass line and I shake my fingers loose and let the cool metal of the guitar strings tease my fingertips. I caress the strings with a couple of light, slow licks and let the notes float over the audience. Then I add some bite, high hollow licks that arc and sing with a tone that both mourns and celebrates. The applause starts again, light at first, then growing to a roar of cheers and whistles.

As we play, I cease to be *Albert the Janitor.* But I'm not that kid from 1968 either. I'm someone in between, someone who finally understands what he's singing about.

The audience reacts the same way to every song, swaying with the music, singing along with us on the journey. We save our hit song for last. When I strum the opening chords of "Best Ever," the place erupts in a full minute of deafening shouts and cheers. During the song, I actually see Nina singing in Diane's place. Still as I remember her, she's wearing her blazing white dress and smiling at me.

At the end of the song, the audience chants *Best, Best, Best.* We have no encore, so we play our hit again. The performance ends with a lights-on standing ovation for the band, and then for me and Marty. We take deep bows that kill my aching back. Marty grins and shouts to me, 'If you'd written fifty more songs, we'd have been bigger than The Beatles.' He wraps an arm around my shoulder and the audience loves it.

I'm the first staff member to arrive at school on Monday. The walls of the empty hallways are still covered with hand-lettered posters promoting the concert. On the janitor office door, I find a scented sheet of pink stationery folded into the jam. The unsigned message is written in a flowing feminine hand. "You're the Best Ever!" I think of Joanne, the way the tears ran down her cheeks when she thanked us after the concert. Friends and well-wishers interrupted us and swept her away before she was done. I sniff the fragrance on the paper again. Joanne is using Nina's scent.

When staff and students begin to arrive, it's obvious that something fundamental has changed. I'm no longer invisible. Now everyone has a greeting, a smile, or a handshake for me, but no one knows the cloud that hovers above me – tomorrow's anniversary of Nina's death.

That night, I dream of her again. This time, we're walking on a moonlit beach with waves rumbling in the distance. I'm weeping because she's leaving me, but my voice makes no sound. She seems oblivious to my pain. Frustrated, I step in front of her, but she walks through me as if I were the ghost instead of her. I wake in the darkness and sniff the air for her scent – desperate for it – but there's nothing. Yet I've never felt Nina's presence so strong.

I don't know what I should be feeling: grateful that some sort of resolution in my head might mean the nightmares are ending, or grieving because Nina may be gone for good.

I call in sick, unable to face people today.

I don't know for certain how to resolve whatever is going on in my head, but I think I know where it can happen.

Unfortunately, my pickup won't start.

I call Marty. 'Hey, my truck's dead, and I need some wheels tonight.'

'Tonight? What for? You got another gig?'

'No, no. It's… personal.'

'I can read a calendar, man. I know it's the anniversary. I can come pick you up at six. How's that?'

'That'll work.'

'Where we goin'?'

'I'll tell you when you get here.'

The cliff face at the Faber Quarry looks like a gigantic iceberg in the moonlight. Marty's pickup creaks and groans its way up the rutted access road with an aching transmission that shudders when he downshifts. His eyes are wide with apprehension. 'Why are we up here, man?'

'I need you to hang with me for another hour.'

The access road hasn't been maintained since we were kids, when the quarry was shut down. The company yard has been a teenage party spot since then, while nature slowly reclaimed the mountain.

Marty rolls down his window and lets the night air sweep over us. It's warm and heavy with the scent of the tangled chaparral that covers the hillside. Ahead, the road is blocked by a pile of loose rocks and broken tree limbs hung with ribbons of yellow caution tape that shift in the breeze. Beyond the roadblock, rainwater has carved a three-foot deep gash across the roadbed. He stops at the ribbons and sets the brake.

'This is getting weird, man,' he says. 'And walkin' around out here in the dark is definitely not healthy.'

'This is where I played my songs for her, Marty.'

He looks confused. 'Okay, but we're on an overgrown mountainside in the dark. Where do you go from here?'

I step down from the pickup.

He climbs out and trudges over to me. 'You're not gonna' do something crazy, are you?'

'No worries.'

He sees the hand tucked into my jacket. 'What's in your pocket? Is that a gun?'

'Why would I bring a gun?'

'Fuck if I know, but I gotta ask.'

'It's a cell phone with a recorder app.'

'You're gonna' record a conversation with a ghost?'

'Good idea, but no. It's got some songs on it.'

'Songs?' Marty's interest rises.

'Let's go,' I say, starting out. I can feel something in the air. An answer of some sort is out here.

Marty follows, stumbling and sliding, nearly dropping his flashlight. 'Wait up. Have you got a flashlight?'

'Yeah, in my pocket for when I need it.' We continue towards a pair of derelict buildings a hundred yards beyond. The Faber Company's office portables were hauled away by creditors, leaving a flat open quarry yard. It's almost unrecognisable now, covered with the thick growth of chaparral. Our shoes crunch on gravel and fifty years of accumulated glass from broken beer bottles. When Nina and I came here, we'd park across the yard from the sheds, over at the cliff. It was a magical spot, where the view of the valley made us feel like we were looking down from heaven.

'This way,' I say, walking into the head-high brush.

'Hey, there's a cliff over there. Remember?'

I push past a rubbery branch that snaps back into Marty's chest.

'Ouch! See, this is the kind of crazy shit I was talkin' about,' he says.

Protecting my face with raised forearms, I continue through the tangle of branches.

Behind me, Marty calls, 'I'm gonna break something out here in the dark. Hold up, Albert. We need to talk.'

But I push on. The answer is out here. I can feel it stronger than ever.

The cool moonlight shows me the way, and for the first time in years I feel a real sense of direction and purpose.

'Wait up, man. I really need to talk to you.' Marty is falling behind, his voice growing distant. He's already winded by the short walk.

I ignore him, knowing that I'm close now. The brush thickens, and the Blue Tones soundtrack begins to play in my head. It's Marty's opening bass line from "Good Days Past." I'm getting close to something. I think there's a faint scent of perfume in the air, Nina's delicate flowery fragrance mixed with the earthy odour of the chaparral. The branches are larger now, more persistent. They're like claws holding me back, keeping the present separate from the past, the living apart from the dead.

The breeze picks up as Marty's calls grow frantic behind me, but I couldn't stop now even if I wanted to.

Then I glimpse movement. Something white. Light and airy, it floats above the stubborn brush. I rush after her, stumbling through the growth, desperate for a clear look. But she teases me, riding the breeze and fluttering away in the moonlight.

Please don't leave. Not now. Not when I'm so close.

A sudden rush of wind sweeps over my face as I part a tangle of branches. I have a momentary glimpse of the distant city lights before my feet slip away. Then I'm on my back, sliding down a short barren slope that I know leads to the edge of the cliff. I claw for a handhold. Brittle roots and twigs snap and tear away in my hands. Then two fingers of my left hand find an exposed root that stops my slide into oblivion.

With both feet dangling over the edge of the precipice, I lay there unmoving. A white plastic shopping bag flutters above me, snagged on a branch. It's a moment of utter and complete clarity. The old band, Nina, the accident, and now my life held suspended by two fingers and a tiny, brittle root. I finally get it.

Above me, Marty comes crashing through the brush. The yellow beam of his flashlight blinds me.

'Jesus, Albert. Can you climb back up? Should I call someone?'

I stare up at the stars and open myself to whatever comes next.

'Hold on, Albert. Oh shit!' Marty's silhouette moves about, jerking with panic and indecision. 'Can you climb up or what?'

'Why'd you push me so hard to play the concert?'

'Jesus. We're friends. We had a band.'

'Come on, Marty, I'm hanging over a cliff here. Give it to me straight. Why? Say it.'

Exasperated, he says, 'You have to ask? After 46 years you have to ask? To get you out of your shell, man. To get your songs out there. It's a second chance, Albert.' And then quietly, 'A second chance for me.'

I look up at the moon and the stars sparkling like scattered diamond chips on a black ceiling. I explore the little root with my fingers and think about how long it's been since I felt in control of my life.

'I just wanted to snap you out of it, Albert. I just wanted... Oh fuck it! Do you want to get your skinny ass back up here or what?'

I see myself lying there on the edge of a cliff with a silly shopping bag waving in the wind above me and say, 'Yeah, I think so.'

A CUT ROCK DOES NOT BLEED, IT SHINES

Shelley Lavigne

I uncover the first gem by peeling my right palm open, tripping over one of my mother's decorative stepping stones.

The ground rushes to meet me with more enthusiasm than my parents ever have and I put my hands out to catch my fall.

At first, there's no pain and, despite the gouges I've made in the path, it seems I've escaped injury. The raw red ache comes only when I turn my hands over and see the damage: deep scarlet gore and torn white skin.

And something strange.

Dug into the meat of my palm, surrounded by black dots of gravel and welling blood is a pea-sized, gleaming blue stone.

I pinch and pull at it – the pain lancing, deep and stubborn, like popping a cystic zit. The skin around the rock turns white, there's more buried in my palm; what I see is just the tip of the iceberg.

The gem is inside me. Unveiled, not implanted by my fall.

It hurts, but I'm relieved. My skin's always felt wrong, my limbs disjointed – a busted animatronic in the wrong flesh suit. But I'd never had a reason to believe that this wasn't just in my head, until now.

Sobs burst out, an unstoppable flow like the blood from my wound; salt and water, confusion and relief.

The door behind me opens.

'Tallia, no!' my mother pulls me inside before the neighbours see me. Our house is the last wartime bungalow on a block bulldozed to make way for modern mini-mansions. The neighbours want to get rid of our "eyesore" – mother's mosaic-covered paving stones be damned – to increase their property values. They send us bylaw officers monthly for various violations; dad calls it death by a thousand fines. My mother insists I behave like a "nice young lady" and not draw their attention. So, no moody outbursts, no boyfriends with modified mufflers (preferably, no boyfriends at all), and always modestly dressed (in my mother's hand-me-downs).

'I'm fine,' I insist.

Regardless, she hauls me into the bathroom and pulls out the first aid kit.

'Let me see.' Her tone is no more soothing than the prickles of alcohol she pours on the abrasions.

Nurse Mother has taken over.

Her trained grip and keen eyes mean I've lost my chance to evade discovery. The stone gleams as rubbing alcohol stings the cut.

She gasps as the red curtain parts.

'Where did you find this?'

'It was on the ground. I didn't steal it, I swear!'

Her face falls, perhaps sensing my lie, but Nurse Mother takes over again. She flicks open the special bright lights she uses to count her wrinkles and pulls open the kit.

The blue in my palm glitters, sparkles.

'This will hurt.'

She grabs the gem with tweezers and pulls. It doesn't come out. I groan but try to keep the crying to a minimum.

She sets down the tweezers and I know from past splinters that the next tool is the scalpel. My mother doesn't like it when I whine but I can't help myself when she puts in a fresh blade. I cradle my hand to my chest and a red smear marks my school uniform. I'll need to clean it later.

'Give,' she commands simply. I look away as she gently cuts the raw tissue in my palm, the pain worse than the alcohol. Tears blur my vision. The stone, as it emerges, is rough, deep blue. She places the gem in the alcohol lid before turning back to me, face drawn.

'Don't tell y—'

'What's going on?' Dad stands in the doorway, framed like a hero. Always good at sensing what is out of place, he spots the blue gem in the cap of alcohol. 'What is this?'

Grinning, he picks up the little cap and tips it out onto his palm, holding the gem up to the light. Cleaned of blood, the uncut gem matches the blue of his widening eyes, as if he holds a copy of his iris between his fingers. Our irises – I've got his eyes.

'It's huge!'

'I'll get it appraised tomorrow,' my mother tells him, hand extended. He places it reverently, reluctantly in her palm.

'I always knew you'd be special too, kid,' he says to me, shadowboxing my chin like when I was younger. It feels awkward but also kind of nice. Loving.

I haven't seen him smile this big in years.

'I'll order us a pizza,' he says as he walks away.

My mother is silent. She seems mad, but she bandages the gaping wound with more care than she usually reserves for my scrapes and bruises.

'I got you a treat,' my mother says, giving me cookies that come packaged with icing for dipping. As a kid, I used to beg for these snacks but she always said no, saying they were expensive and unhealthy.

The rock fetched a good price; this is my reward.

She rubs my back while we watch TV, something she hasn't done in years. She goes slowly, meticulously. I melt into it until I realise she is assessing whether the raised spots on my skin are acne or shallowly buried gems.

But the acne never grows enough to warrant closer investigation and the cookies are eaten and not replenished.

Back rubs evolve into a kind of pat down and then fade away completely.

The small scar on my palm heals into a thin white line. There's no dent, no evidence of the treasure that was under my skin, that I incubated.

No evidence of the part of me that was taken away.

I shouldn't miss it. It's not like I needed it.

It's better this way.

For all of us.

She looks at my report card as if it is a tarot spread. The future looks B for Bleak.

I scratch a painful lump an inch below my elbow.

'Are you even trying?'

I nod. Of course I am. I always finish my homework, read the textbooks, do the practice tests. But faced with the real thing – the first year this really matters – I froze, crushed under the weight of expectations. Crushed under pressure.

'It's hard out there, you need to take this seriously. You won't get into medical school without getting into a good university. And you can't get into a good university without good grades.' My mother sighs. 'We've been over this.'

We have. The path from good grades to a "bright" future is so well-worn that correlation has become causation in my mother's mind.

I want to tell her to get a life of her own and stop living mine, but she'll lash out and nothing will change. Instead, I scratch my arm harder, feeling the tip of my finger wetten. I've burrowed through my epidermis. See, I know things. What kind of sixteen-year-old calls their skin epidermis? The kind that gets mercilessly teased at school.

The texture under my nails turns rough, hard.

Another one.

I thought it was just eczema.

I flinch and hide my arm behind my back; the motion alerts my mother. She grabs my arm, twisting it until the underside is exposed.

'Another?'

I am pulled to the bathroom, ministered with the first aid kit. 'Hold still.'

Skin parts like an overstuffed omelette as she drags the tip of the scalpel along. The kidney-bean-sized blue gem falls with a clank on the linoleum and I feel relief, a release of pressure, followed by grief at its loss. It's even bigger than my first, more valuable. And it's proof that the last one wasn't a fluke, that I am a steady source of these beautiful gems.

I want to hold it – keep it, after all, there will be others for them to sell – but my dad practically leaps on it.

'You're really remarkable.' He ruffles my hair, pocketing the gem before wandering off. He's forgiven my report card failings; the gems are a much better promise for my future than grades ever could be. But my mother is still frowning.

She takes out the alcohol and the stack of bandaids, measuring them against the hole in my arm until she finds one big enough. It's a problem she knows she can solve. She's so focused, and seems to be enjoying this.

That's the thing with nursing, it walks the fine line between healing and causing pain.

'We just want you to have a good, stable job. Dad and I won't be able to support you forever.' Are the gems not enough? What more do I need to do to make her happy? Can she even feel happiness? She looked happy in pictures of us when I was a newborn, still covered in blood and juices. Was that woman different from the one who stands in front of me today?

I pull my arm from her grasp and stomp to my bedroom, slamming the door behind me.

I know what I want to do, even if I promised myself I would never do it again. The vent in the corner of my room eyes me like a painting, begging me to retrieve what I've hidden inside.

I sit on my bed making a pros and cons list until midnight, when I hear my father's snores through the wall – they'll cover any noise I might make.

My actions are compulsion rather than choice, like a starving person eating until they vomit. I remove the vent cover, carefully pulling out my little plastic bag and old spoon. I haven't seen it in a while but, like an old friend, I recognise the dents from the times it scraped rock and the crooked bend of its head.

I feel the hot tangle of shame in my belly – I am weak, I am dirt – as I place the hot dented metal in my mouth. The comforting weight of the spoon, the familiarity of it, balances out the shame. For now.

I creep downstairs and into our yard, kneeling in the dirt.

I fill the spoon, placing it in my mouth, the dirt turning to mud and coating the moist surfaces wherein. I'd forgotten the slight chocolate taste and the fizzing feeling. I chew to moisten what I've packed in my mouth, falling back on my haunches in delight. Palming at the soil with my hands, I shove more of the loam into my mouth.

The motion-activated light in the neighbour's backyard turns on and their dog starts barking. I nearly throw the spoon, like a criminal disposing of a murder weapon.

This is bad.

This is bad.

My mother is a light sleeper and, sure enough, I see the glow of her window projected onto the lawn. There is no way she won't go look outside. I panic at the threat of discovery – my face is covered in dirt and shame. She'd know I've been at it again.

I press myself into the darkest corner of the yard and wait a couple minutes after her light goes out for her to go back to sleep before creeping back indoors, shaking from the close call but also pleasantly full.

I suck on my fingers until even the nails are clean and white.

I sleep like a baby.

The next gem appears two weeks later, pressing on the stress knot near my right shoulder during a gym test.

'I've always said you'd do great things,' my father says, holding my hand and telling me to squeeze when it hurts as my mother cuts into my skin. I cry, and it's not just because of the pain.

That night, the main character in the movie we're watching wears a giant blue sapphire necklace and I feel a fresh pang for every gem I've lost. Was it hers, one that she got to keep?

It's beautiful, large, and a deep blue.

What kind of pain grew a gem like that?

The next one comes six days later when they announce the ladies' choice winter prom and Josh, who sits next to me in class and does group projects with me, insists that I ask him.

'It's my choice,' I tell him.

'I know, that's what makes it more meaningful.'

My mother listens to my story with a gleam of pride while cutting out a gem four inches down from my collarbone. I hope it's because I stood up for myself, choosing to focus on my studies and avoid romance until after med school, the one rule we do agree on. But instead, she says, 'We'll have to find you a dress with a neckline that covers the wound.'

She wastes no time, telling dad we'll be out doing "girly things" and nearly breaks the speed limit to get us to the mall. Once there, she takes me to the places we usually can't afford, pointing out dresses she would have worn if she were my age. I'm in a daze until she holds up a rather awful pink number against my body and I realise the gems will be paying for it. This is the last way I'd want to spend the money.

'Why don't you just go instead?' I yell, taking refuge in the changing rooms.

The rings of the curtain give a protesting squeak as I draw them shut between us, but they don't pack the punch of slamming a door.

The pain of the new gem crystalizing above my knee lances as I wind back to kick the wall. Full of grace, I fall backwards into a mass of glitter and taffeta.

'Hey, can I come in?' My mother's voice is softer than usual, like she's soothing a distressed patient.

'Sign says one person per room.'

'I won't tell them if you don't.'

I chuckle despite myself and she takes it as permission to enter. I stop rubbing my knee but not fast enough and her eyes catch the movement. At least there's no first aid kit here; I'll have a reprieve. With any luck, she'll forget by the time we get home.

She sits down beside me on the ground, staring at my knee silently.

'Why do you want me to go to the dance so badly?' I ask when the silence becomes too much.

'Don't you want to go?'

'No.'

'You should! You'll have fun. I regret not doing this stuff as a kid. I was way too focused on school.' I want to point out the irony to her. 'You only get one childhood, appreciate it. Live a little. Life gets hard when you're older.'

'And why don't *you* live a little, mom?'

'I tried – it nearly killed me.' I open my mouth to ask questions but she shakes her head. 'You're much stronger and smarter than I ever was – you get it from your dad. You'll just have to live for the both of us.'

That is a lot of responsibility, a lot of pressure. To live out her dreams. And mine too, I guess. If I ever get a chance to figure out what they might look like.

I take her offered hand as she stands.

'Don't tell dad about this conversation and I won't tell him about this.' She points to the bulge on top of my knee. 'I know you want to keep them.'

I nearly cry but instead I nod.

In trying to kick the habit again, I lick the spoon's sharp edges, hoping there might be some molecule of dirt in its crevices. All I can taste is coppery blood as the silver cuts my tongue.

It would help to fill my stomach again, replenish the dark rich core of me. But once I feel satiated, the shame always follows. This taste of blood is as good as it's going to get.

The painful lump above my knee has become a second kneecap and the skin around it is red and inflamed. I am not sure if leaving it alone is the right thing to do, but I wanted this; it's the first thing I've really wanted for myself. If I pull it out, then maybe I don't know myself at all. Maybe it means I'm better off letting my parents decide my future for me.

The light in the hall flashes, snapping me out of my pity party.

The bathroom door squeaks.

I roll over in bed, thinking someone is just peeing. But the rock in my leg twinges and I know I need to be alert. I hear the all too familiar sound of the first aid kit's zip and creep over to the door. Opening it a sliver, I press my eye to the opening.

My mother straddles the toilet, facing away, pyjama top lifted over her shoulders while my father stands behind her.

'Did you disinfect it?' she asks.

'Jesus, Nan. This isn't my first rodeo.'

My father shifts and I see his pocket knife; the same one he uses to cut apples on picnics and open stubborn packages. The one he sharpens in the garage on the first weekend of every month. It slices through my mother's shoulder blade like a knife in butter. My mother doesn't even flinch as he parts the skin with his thumb and index and pulls out a gem.

Hers are so much paler than mine. For a delirious moment, I want to shout a victorious "ha!" and humiliate my mother.

But then I realise what this means – I am not alone.

And that my mother has lied to me.

I look back up at her. Our eyes meet over her shoulder and she smiles sadly.

'It's good that you can still make these in case we need a backup,' my father says, patting her on her other shoulder. I notice a scar there too. And all over her back.

'You're limping,' my father tells me as I broom on Sunday chore day.

It is growing harder to ignore the painful lump. When I touched it this morning, I felt a smaller cluster of gems around it.

'I hit it in gym class. It's just a bruise.'

'Have your mom look at it.'

His delivery is automatic, as if he doesn't understand the implications and I think I might be saved until my mother enters the room, summoned by my liar's karma, hands full of flyers to sort.

'What is it?'

'Your daughter is hurt.'

'She's fine.'

This is a mistake – he knows she always jumps at the opportunity to nurse me, keep her "skills" sharp. I've never had a bump or a bruise she hasn't peered deeply at, never been prescribed a drug she didn't scrutinise.

'But you didn't even look at it,' my father insists.

'She looked at it yesterday,' I say.

'It was fine. Just a cut.' She rips out a coupon.

'A cut? Natallia said it was a bruise.'

'It's a cut and a bruise.' I try. It's no use. The damage is done. My dad is no idiot. When he turns to me, his face is splotchy with rage.

'Are you growing an uncultured gem? Do you have any idea how dangerous that is? I thought you'd be smart enough to figure that out without me needing to spell it out for you. And you–' He turns to my mother. I am acutely aware of the outline of the knife in his back pocket as his tone rises and hands shake. A flash of last night's dream – him stabbing my mother in the back repeatedly, the knife sparking as it hit the stones hidden just under the surface – hits me like *déja vu*. 'You knew about this and encouraged it? What happened when you hid your gems from me, huh? They spread like cancer – you nearly *died.* You couldn't work, I had to support the both of us on my measly salary. And I never once complained because I love you. I even gave you a kid, against my better judgement, because you

209

said you needed purpose when you couldn't work anymore. And this is how you repay me? Endangering our child?'

He reaches into his back pocket and I try to hold back his arm but only brush his sleeve.

He hands my mother his knife.

'Take care of your mess.'

My skin itches under the bandaid. I'm healing fine, although the sight of the black thread and the inch-long incision gave me the creeps when my mother changed the dressing this morning.

I flip absentmindedly through the biology textbook and land on the page about evolution and the fossil record. Long-dead animals trapped under mounds of dirt, their bones slowly turning into rock as calcium is replaced by other minerals.

At least they got to turn into stone only after they died. They didn't have parts of themselves scattered to the four winds to pay the bills.

I wander at lunch and my feet take me to the library. I delay the inevitable, and stand pondering in the fiction section for a couple minutes before going to my true destination, the geology section: 550.

There are three types of rock: sedimentary (like fossils), igneous (from volcanoes) and metamorphic. This last type is created by great pressures under the crust of the earth.

Geological forces can turn a stone into a precious gem. And gems can be subjected to stronger geological forces and become something else.

Something else entirely.

The motion-activated light in my neighbour's yard doesn't turn on as I step outside – I clipped the cable after school.

I head to the back corner of our yard, the muddy mess my dad always plans to resod but never does.

It's perfect.

I kneel in the mud and scrape my hands in the dirt. It's tempting to satisfy my cravings but I focus on the task at hand. Soon I'll have as much to eat as I could ever want. So, I dig and dig, arms shaking. I should have worked harder in gym class.

Rocks and debris cut at my fingers, pull at my nails, but still I dig. Even if I start to bleed.

The moon rises over the fenceline and lights the scene in silver.

I sit back and see my fingers gleaming in the moonlight.

The tips of my fingers have worn away, revealing an opalescent swirl of colours where bones should be. I peel back skin like wrapping paper; it hurts until it's completely removed, then I just feel the cool soft night on my glimmering bones.

They're even more beautiful than the gems.

Wonder turns to dread – if my parents learn about this, I'm worried they'll pull my bones out of me to sell. I doubt I can grow back a bone the way the gem polyps regrow.

A hand closes over my mouth.

'It's me,' my mother whispers before I can protest.

I look back and notice she's holding the de-icing shovel.

'It took me a while to find this,' she says, handing it to me.

She glances at my hands but says nothing, grabbing a trowel and digging.

'You're okay with this?' I ask.

'Once you've made up your mind, I can't change it. Like your dad.' I've always thought of her as the stubborn one. 'It's not what I would have chosen.'

No, I've seen what she chose and I do not want it. I grab the shovel and kick it into the dirt, heaving out the heavy dark brown soil. My mother works hard next to me, making up for tool size with gusto. She'd been strong once, enough to lift patients, and she still has ropy muscle.

The moon lazily travels across the sky as we sweat and work.

The sky is lightening by the time the hole is a couple feet deep and long enough for me to curl up into. It isn't as deep as I wanted but it will do the trick. I can burrow deeper later.

There isn't much time left.

I look over at mom, at her smiling muddy face. Sweat has cleaned a line around her forehead. I've never seen her look this exhilarated.

'Come with me.' I don't let myself think about the implications of this before I say it. About the complicated way I both desperately want her to say yes, but hope she says no.

Mom shakes her head and takes my hands in hers, cleaning the mineral tips now covered in dirt.

'I can't. Someone has to take care of your dad.'

'You're staying for *him*? Really?'

'He took care of me, gave me support and hid my secret from those who would have wanted to take me apart and study me. He let me quit my job when the stress of it was too much. Even though it meant we'd never have it easy, couldn't afford fancy vacations or have a comfortable retirement. And he gave me you.'

'He takes the gems away. He hurts you – us.'

'Nothing is ever perfect.'

I want to yell at her, not just for being an idiot but also for everything she has done, how she used me, how selfish she's been. How she's staying in a situation so unhappy she has to live out her life through others. But I don't want those parting words echoing in her memory.

She presents me with dad's knife. I wonder how many times it's cut her.

I plunge it into my belly button, opening myself up. The metal sparks as it scrapes my mineral core. It hurts. It hurts so much more than any cut mom ever gave me, hurts so bad I stop.

But her hands join mine, pulling when mine falter. We stop at my chin as I bite back a scream.

Together, we peel back my skin, slough off my former epidermis. As it disconnects from my true core, I no longer feel any pain at all, only the soothing kiss of silver moonlight along my gleaming bones and pumping organs. I look down at the hollow flesh sac, the gory mess of skin, blood, fat and hair abandoned on the ground. It doesn't feel like mine, it never has.

Maybe I'll grow something new eventually; already I can see the gem polyps forming around my bones.

Mom weeps, reaching out to trace a finger along my opalescent ribs. Is this what she looks like on the inside too?

'You're beautiful, you know?'

She is too, in spite of everything.

'I love you,' she says, and holds my hands, helping me descend into the ground. I finally move freely, as if my skin had been rubber bands holding me in a state of tension. I could jump into the sky, but instead I curl up in my cradle of mud.

Her tears fall and dampen the dirt she shovels over me. I keep my gem-blue eyes fixed on her until they are covered.

The dirt presses down on me, her final hug. I feel her pat the ground when she's done, saying goodbye.

Soon, I'll burrow deeper. But I will give myself a day to say goodbye before my new life begins.

A day to see if she'll follow.

THE NEW CALEDONIAN

Tony Dunnell

'Stubborn bloody thing,' said Natasha, peeling the link strip from the shaved side of her head. She sat up in the padded orthodontic chair and rubbed her eyes as they readjusted to the whiteness of the small research laboratory.

'Maybe the neural AI can't figure him out yet,' said Kezia, immersed in the code on her computer screens. 'We knew it would be tricky with a bird.'

Natasha rose from the chair and stepped to the window into Clive's small, white-walled enclosure. The crow was sitting on a single bare branch suspended from the ceiling. He stared at Natasha. His soft head feathers had grown back to cover the delicate implant attached to his skull. Despite her frustration with the experiment, she still admired the sleek New Caledonian crow.

They had spent much of the last month together, in the large, mesh-enclosed aviary in the research facility's park, which Clive returned to after his daily periods of free flight. He had accepted her presence within days, with the help of insects, snails and other treats. He solved puzzles, his causal reasoning showing swift improvements. When he struggled with a complex task, Natasha solved it for him. He learned by watching. Cause and effect, cue and criterion. Clive was a clever bird.

After a month, they thought Clive was ready; but three days and three link attempts later, the connection remained a blurry blackness.

Natasha put her hand flat against the glass of Clive's window. The bird cocked his head and watched as Natasha talked to Kezia. 'You know when you wake up from a dream, and you know something happened but all that's left is a vague emotion, no images or memory? It's kind of like that. Hollow. Not like the others at all.'

Kezia walked over and joined Natasha at the window.

'Maybe he's shy, Nat,' said Kezia. 'Your new punk hairdo is kind of intimidating.'

'Shut up,' said Natasha, laughing, instinctively running a hand through the short wave of brown hair that covered the top of her otherwise shaved head. 'It's practical.'

'It suits you.'

'The new me, right? Thirty-something punk scientist seeks companion. Must be willing to share life with reluctant crow.' Natasha pushed the feeder button on the wall. Nuts and seeds scattered out onto the wooden platform below Clive's perch. The crow hopped down and pecked at the treats, his silky blackness in sharp contrast to the white walls. 'Let's shut things down, it's late. I'll take him back to the aviary.'

Natasha boarded the King's Cross hyperloop back to her home in Edinburgh. The pod was full of suited commuters sliding briefcases into overhead compartments. She dropped onto a vacant window seat. The virtual window displayed a simple map of the thirty-minute route from London to Edinburgh. She shut her eyes, but her mind was too active for sleep.

Someone sat in the aisle seat beside her. She opened her eyes and glanced over. One of the suits, smelling of a woody cologne. The lights dimmed to a deep pink and the pod began to accelerate.

'Hello,' said the suit as he settled into his chair.

'Hi.' Natasha sat up and slid her laptop out of the backpack at her feet. She placed it on the fold-out table in front of her. She opened the laptop and stared at the screen, then closed it with a sigh.

'Long day?' asked the man. The smile lines around his eyes hinted at the approach of middle age. His hair was short and black, his stubble flecked with grey.

'Yeah, long day,' said Natasha.

'I've seen you on TV. Talking to the animals.'

'Ah, yes, the amazing Doctor Dolittle.'

The man laughed. 'I'm Andrew.'

'Natasha.'

'Nice to meet you, Natasha. But I'll shut up now. I know the annoyance of talkative strangers on the loop.' He leaned back into his seat and shut his eyes.

His face was kind and rugged. A slender scar marked his temple. 'It's okay,' said Natasha, 'I'll only be thinking about work anyway.'

Andrew angled his head toward her. 'Not going well?'

'Not great. I'm having problems connecting.'

'Aren't we all?' he said, smiling. 'My dog seems to understand me, I guess, but he's kind of stupid.'

Natasha laughed and a rare thought crossed her mind: *Is he flirting? Hell, am I?* The thought unsettled her, so she continued talking. 'We're attempting a neural link with a bird, which was probably a bad idea. No neocortex.'

'Ah, yes,' said Andrew, 'the old neocortex. What's that in layman's terms?'

'Sorry, habit. It's the part of the brain that deals with cognition and sensory perception. Stuff like that. And language, in humans. Birds don't have one.'

'Birds, eh? Strange creatures.' Andrew's phone rang. 'Sorry, work.'

Natasha tried – and failed – not to listen as Andrew chatted to someone called Mike about 3D modelling, space and "the concept." Natasha decided that Andrew was an architect.

'Sorry about that,' said Andrew when the call ended.

'No problem.'

A note chimed in the pod, followed by a smooth, automated female voice. *We are now approaching Manchester. We will arrive in Manchester in one minute. One minute.*

'That's me,' said Andrew. He smiled and extended his hand. 'Nice to meet you, Natasha. Good luck with the birds.'

Natasha shook his hand. 'Nice to meet you, too. Good luck with... connecting.'

Andrew laughed. He stood and pulled his case from the overhead compartment as the pod glided to a stop. The doors opened and the sounds of the station flooded in. 'Take care,' he said. He turned, walked down the aisle and stepped outside. The door slid shut behind him.

Natasha was home by 10 pm. She stepped out of the autocab and walked up the garden path. The ground floor lights were on, which meant her daughter was home and still up. She smiled.

'Hi, mum,' said Amy as Natasha entered. Amy was sat on the living room sofa watching a film, which she paused while Natasha hung up her jacket. 'Dad just dropped me off. Did you see him?'

'No, must have just missed him.'

'He told me to tell you that he's going to Vancouver next weekend, so is it okay if I stay with you?'

'Of course, he knows that.' John was always asking stupid questions.

'How did it go with Clive?' asked Amy. 'Did you get more than caw caws?'

'Nothing. A lot of staring. I can feel him, but he won't engage. I can't figure out what he wants.'

Natasha went to the adjoining kitchen and poured herself a glass of merlot. She opened the fridge and took out a bowl of last night's pasta.

Amy joined Natasha in the kitchen. 'Maybe he doesn't want anything, mum.'

'Maybe, honey.' Natasha drank the last of her wine and returned the pasta to the fridge. 'Do you mind if I go to bed? I'd love to stay up longer, but I'm shattered.'

'Okay. Night, mum.'

'Night, honey.' She kissed Amy's forehead.

Natasha walked upstairs to her bedroom. 'Lights.' The bedroom lights came on, soft and calming. 'Shower.' Natasha undressed, entered the steam-filled ensuite bathroom and stepped into the shower. She shut her eyes and let the warm water stream into her mouth and down her body. Her mind raced. Amy and John. The man on the train. The blackness of the neural link. Hollow. *Why do we have trouble connecting?* She ran her fingertips through her crop of wet hair. Her thumb passed over the implant that lay under the skin of her right temple.

Why couldn't she connect with the crow? The world had been amazed by Tatiana the Dolphin and Arnold the Chimpanzee. The conversations, as basic as they were, had gone viral. Natasha had spent weeks doing interviews. The real-life Doctor Doolittle, that's what the tabloids called her. It was a welcome distraction after the death of her sister and the relief that followed, and the guilt of that relief. The guilt had grown.

Natasha stepped out of the shower. She dried herself with a green towel then wrapped it around her body. In the bathroom mirror, her reflection lay buried beneath condensation. She drew a finger across the fog where her eyes would be. Green eyes looked back at her. She turned away.

Natasha and Kezia spent most of the next day in the laboratory expanding the translative web. It was repetitive, but Kezia was happy to feed the AI every possible pathway. Natasha and Clive played image-matching games interspersed with video and audio clips: images of seeds and sky, sounds of car horns and rain. Kezia watched the AI spin its strands, extending its mesh of feelings, of analogous reasoning. The dark sparks of human and corvid minds, unconnected but overlapping. Clive was rewarded with treats. Natasha and Kezia ate M&M's.

At 5:45 pm., they decided to run the neural link again.

Kezia checked the connection and primed the AI. 'Comfortable?'

'Comfortable.' Natasha sat back in her seat, shut her eyes and waited for the connection.

'In five... three, two, one. Connection active.'

Natasha exhaled and let the neural link wash through her consciousness. She enjoyed the sensation, like diving into a pool of honey and being sucked through into weightlessness. From there, it depended on the species and the subject.

The connection stabilised. Natasha cleared her mind before searching out Clive's presence in the dark. She thought of a greeting, *Hello, Clive,* and the words appeared in white letters that floated away across the black plain on which Natasha's consciousness stood.

What do you want, Clive? The thought was meant for herself alone, not for the crow, and she immediately checked herself. She couldn't allow yesterday's frustrations to bleed over into this fourth session. She tried to sink further into a void state, letting her mind drift in the darkness. As she drifted, a memory of her sister surfaced. Her smile, the smell of the hospital. A flicker of panic. It was exactly what she was trying to avoid.

Suspicion. It flooded around her, calm but palpable. That was new. Disconcerting, but new at least.

Hello, Clive, thought Natasha, and again the words appeared and drifted away. She waited in the dark, listening to her own breathing. A flicker in the distance. A sound, *flit flit,* and a dancing shadow. The suspicion subsided and Natasha's world rotated. Shadowy, swirling clouds came from the dark, *flit flit,* and wrapped around her like smoke. The crow emerged, his head huge and dominating, his beak a blade between intense black eyes, an inch from Natasha's mental perspective. He stared, fixed on Natasha's consciousness. She resisted the urge to call out for a disconnection.

Clive.

Clive is here.

Natasha couldn't tell which thoughts were her own as the crow enveloped her and she disappeared into the ink of his eye. Images blinked and flickered all around her, like an old movie reel flashing fragments of memories on the walls of her mind.

The whirl stopped and Amy appeared. In the kitchen, at home. 'Maybe he doesn't want anything, mum,' she said.

'Maybe, honey.'

I want nothing. I want for nothing.

Change. Natasha saw herself from high above, walking across the research facility park beneath the winter sun, a week or so ago. The perspective dived, sending cold ripples through Natasha's body. The grass rushed up, each blade close and trembling, alive and sharp. Elastic movement. She catapulted upwards, a rush of brown-gold leaves and black branches inches from her eyes, and then through to the overwhelming brightness of the sky. No misgiving, no fear, a pure celebration in the freedom of flying. Above the city, above the trapped world.

Change. Her sister lay dying. She smiled at Natasha from the hospital bed, her blue eyes shining. Fresh flowers in a vase, cards with hearts, white sheets.

'Don't worry, yeah, sis?' She was so thin, but so radiant still. She reached out, took Natasha's hand and squeezed it. 'Just be happy, okay?' A tear rolled down Natasha's cheek. 'For me, yeah? Promise?'

'Promise,' said Natasha.

The image faded and Natasha was back in the dark, alone and floating. It was peaceful, wonderfully so, a hopeful space between heartbeats.

A synthesis.

Family? Clive was all around her, within her, blurring the lines between them.

Yes, family.

Gone.

Yes, gone.

You are good.

You are good, too.

I am crow.

Yes.

I want for nothing.

I know.

What do you want?

Natasha didn't know how to answer. She thought of Amy. Of getting home late from work and seeing the lights still on. She thought of her sister, unrestricted, and the relief of knowing she was at peace. Thankful. No, not thankful. Free. Of the burden, the responsibility, the guilt.

Freedom, they thought. *We are crow.*

The blackness rolled. 'Natasha?' Dancing phosphenes sparked in Natasha's eyes. 'Nat? Nat?' Kezia's voice came quick and concerned.

Natasha opened her eyes. Kezia's face was close, a blur in the light of the laboratory. 'Kez?' said Natasha, her voice slight.

'You're crying, Nat. And your patterns are all over the place. I cut the link. What the hell happened?'

'He was inside me, Kez, right here.' She touched her fingers to her brow. 'He's happy, Kez. So perfectly content. It felt like... like childhood.'

'Stay in your seat, okay?' said Kezia, gently pulling the link strip from Natasha's temple. 'Don't get up.'

Clive was perched on his branch behind the glass of the enclosure, his eyes fixed on Natasha. Kezia went back to the computer and Natasha pushed herself up from the chair and stepped to the enclosure window. She placed her hands flat on the glass. The room shuddered and Natasha swayed.

'Jesus, Nat,' said Kezia, and Natasha felt her friend's arms wrap around her as she blacked out.

Natasha opened her eyes to the flat of the ceiling. She was lying down. Kezia was there with Aarnav, a fellow researcher at the facility. 'What happened?' she asked.

She had fainted, they explained, and passed out for a few seconds. Kezia had called Aarnav, who was working late, and they helped her walk to the nap room.

'How's Clive?' said Natasha, sitting up on the bed.

'He seemed confused. Didn't eat,' said Kezia. 'I took him back to the aviary. More importantly, how are you? You've been asleep for twenty minutes. We were about to call a doctor.'

'I'm good, I think.'

'Maybe you should stay here tonight,' said Aarnav. 'I'm pulling an all-nighter. I can check on you.'

'Thanks, Aarnav, but I'm okay. What did we get from the connection, Kez?'

Kezia rolled her eyes. 'I haven't even looked yet. I've been hauling your bony arse around, and Clive's. Tomorrow, okay? It's getting late. I'll call you a taxi, if you're sure you're alright.'

Natasha stood among the flow of people beneath the lofty, vaulted roof of King's Cross hyperloop station. The sounds were incessant, like insects. Footsteps, the clatter of wheeled luggage, the laughter of young men and women. The smell of coffee and perfume. She stood and breathed it in.

A young woman bumped into Natasha's shoulder and apologised. Natasha moved, walked to where she needed to be, to the platform that took her home. The people moved with her.

'Natasha.'

A pod arrived and the strangers around her readied themselves. They hoisted bags and shuffled their feet, trained to the routine. Get on, get off; be here, be there.

'Natasha.'

225

A hand touched her shoulder. She turned. It was the man, Andrew.

'Natasha. I was hoping I might see you.' People flowed around them. A hive of humanity. So much movement, jostling for space. 'Shall we get on?'

Natasha boarded the pod and Andrew followed behind her. They sat next to each other, Andrew in the aisle seat again, Natasha with her backpack at her feet. The lights dimmed to pink and the capsule left the station.

'Sorry,' said Andrew. 'I hope I didn't startle you. I was buying a newspaper in the station and saw you.'

'It's okay,' said Natasha.

'How's work?' he asked.

'It's okay.' Natasha's head was heavy. She rested it on Andrew's shoulder. 'Do you mind? I'm so tired.'

'No. No, of course not.'

Natasha closed her eyes. Every movement made a sound, and every sound a movement. The rush of the capsule. The rise and fall of Andrew's breathing. The chatter of passengers and the turning of newspaper pages. One could be so present, and so gone.

Natasha dreamed.

Aarnav was outside the aviary. The stars were fading in the swirl of his cigarette smoke. The silver-blue nicotine cloud formed a dolphin, and it curled around the moon. The moon stuttered and the world folded into itself, into the shadows.

They slept, with black wings wrapped around them.

'Natasha. Natasha, we're here.'

Natasha opened her eyes. 'Where?'

'Edinburgh,' said Andrew. 'You were fast asleep. I didn't want to wake you. Come on, I'll get you a taxi and then I'll head back to Manchester. Don't forget your bag.'

Natasha grabbed her backpack and followed Andrew down the aisle. They stepped out into the noise of the station, crossed the platform and walked up the stairs to Princes Street. Outside, the night air was cold and cutting and full of lights and life.

'Damn, it's cold,' said Andrew. 'Are you hungry? We could–'

'Yes,' said Natasha. She shook her head, touched her fingers to her temple, then looked up into Andrew's eyes. 'I mean, sorry, I have to get home.'

'Sure.' His eyes glinted in the streetlights. 'Are you okay?'

'Yeah. Sorry, I'm just really tired.'

'Some other time, maybe. Get some rest. Shall I call you a taxi? It's freezing out here.'

'No, it's okay. Get back on the loop.'

'Here, take my card. Just, you know, in case.'

'Thanks, Andrew.' Natasha took the card and walked away. Lights and buses and bicycles streaked along Princes Street. People sat and ate, some laughing, some holding hands, behind glittering panes of glass. Sirens and car horns hung in the air. Natasha walked beneath a scaffold that clung to the façade of a shop like a parasite. The shop was closed, but in the dark of its window the curved bodies of violins and guitars slid in and out of view in the headlight of passing cars. Natasha caught her reflection in the glass. Her face was a shadow cast by neon lights.

Natasha flagged down a taxi and got inside. It was warm.

'Where to, love?' asked the driver. His face was round and ruddy. She told him her address, sat back and shut her eyes.

'Thanks,' said Natasha when they arrived. She paid the driver and stepped out of the taxi. She walked up the garden path. The ground floor lights were on, which meant her daughter was home.

It was warm inside. Natasha hung up her jacket. Amy wasn't in the living room, so she went upstairs to the girl's bedroom. The door was open. The bedside light cast a yellow halo over the girl on the bed. Natasha walked in and sat beside her sleeping daughter.

'Hi, mum,' Amy murmured, then drifted back to sleep.

Natasha placed a hand on the girl's brown hair, which was smooth above her skull and glistened in the light. She removed her hand, as if it didn't belong there.

Her daughter. Family. How had she arrived here? She remembered being alone and free, and walking drunk in the wind, kissing friends and lovers.

Is this your family?

Yes.

It is small.

Yes.

Where have they gone?

Just gone. Apart from Amy.

Natasha lay down beside her daughter. Amy's hair smelled like fields after rain, and blackberries, and arguments. Natasha fell asleep.

'Mum? Mum? Are you alright? It's freezing out here.'

Natasha was standing at the bottom of the back garden, clothed but barefoot. The grass was cold and damp. The sounds of the city floated over her, beneath the slate of the open sky.

'Mum!'

Natasha turned toward the house. Amy was standing in the back doorway, her arms wrapped across her chest. She put on some shoes and came across the grass toward Natasha.

'Why are you out here?' said Amy. She took Natasha's hand. 'Bloody hell, mum, you're freezing.'

'Look at the sky,' said Natasha.

'Mum, what's wrong? You're being weird. Have you taken something?'

Natasha smiled. 'I remember when I was a girl. Before everything.' She frowned. 'Why do we have trouble connecting?'

'Screw this,' said Amy. She pulled her phone out of the front pocket of her sweater and tapped at the screen. She put the phone to her ear, her eyes fixed on Natasha. 'Hi, Kez, this is Amy... Yeah. Well, no. I'm with mum. She's acting strange. We're in the garden... I don't know... Okay.' Amy held out the phone to Natasha. 'Kezia wants to talk to you.'

Natasha took the phone. 'Hi, Kez.'

'Nat, what's going on?' came the voice over the phone.

'Nothing. We're just standing. Look, Kez. Look at the sky.'

'Nat, did Aarnav call you?'

'Aarnav?'

'About Clive. Clive's dead, Nat. Aarnav says he went crazy last night, flying into the mesh. I'm sorry, Nat.'

Natasha inhaled cold air through her nose. The grass between her toes was sharp and wet. 'Clive's not dead.'

'Nat?'

'Clive's here, with me.'

'Natasha, what are you talking about?'

'Look at the sky.'

'Natasha, pass the phone back to Amy.'

She handed the phone back to her daughter, who had tears running down her cheeks. Amy spoke with Kezia again. 'Okay, I will... Be quick, please... Bye, Kez.' Amy hung up, wiped the tears from her face, and took her mother's hand.

Dogs are emotional. They know us instinctively. It's strange, that bond, until you imagine the time involved. Tens of thousands of years. The half-life of plutonium-239. Side by side with humans, for millennia, watching each other.

Clive, on the other hand, had far more in common with maniraptorans than with humankind. Mesozoic. Tens of millions of years ago. And yet, here they were.

In the black, Natasha wondered, without fear, where their body began and where it ended. Their proprioception, their kinaesthesis, seemed non-existent yet endless. But they could hear the voices.

It's not ethical, Kezia.

We're way beyond ethical, Aarnav. This is about saving Nat. Amy's downstairs waiting to see her mother again. I don't see any other options. Honestly, you don't need to be here, I can handle it. You've done enough already.

Even if it works, and we don't kill her, what do we do? Go public? Cover it up?

I don't know, Aarnav. We keep it quiet. We end up in prison, or on the cover of Time. *I don't know, but I have to do this.*

Shit... Let's do it, then.

The void shuddered and a plane formed below what was now Natasha-Clive. A cube of light appeared far below them on the plane. The cube began to move, growing in speed and size until it reached them, until they rushed through it, into a world of light and colour. Green, blue, sun, squares. The aviary in the facility park.

Natasha knew it was artificial. Clive, she sensed, did not.

She reached out and touched the aviary's metal frame. She ran her fingers over the mesh enclosure. It felt real.

'Natasha.'

Turning around, she saw Kezia. She was standing on the grass. An avatar, too clean and precise to be real.

'Hello, Kezia.'

'Hi, Nat. Do you know where we are?'

'This is the aviary,' said Natasha, 'in the park. But not real.'

'Aarnav built it. How are you feeling?'

'We're fine. How are you?'

'Nat, we're at your house, in your bedroom. Amy is downstairs, waiting for you. We have to separate you from Clive. Your brain can't take it. We need to put him back in the aviary, like we do every night. He'll be fine here.'

'Clive is with me,' said Natasha, looking at the sky. 'We are happy.'

'No, Nat. Amy needs you.' Kezia came closer. 'Clive will be happy here. He can't stay with you.'

'Amy can come. No one else has to leave. We'll stay here, together. Happy.'

Kezia stood in silence, considering. 'Aarnav, go ahead.'

In the unreal sky, the clouds began to dissipate and darken. Pinks cut through the blue, then orange and red, and all above became a starless night. A moon rose from the horizon, too large and too close. Cries came from the silhouettes of trees, *caw caw, caw caw*, and a crow came from the black and landed on the aviary. It made its way inside, passing through the wire. More crows descended, until five or six sat inside the dark aviary, a night roost of rustling, jet-black New Caledonians.

'Clive,' said Kezia, 'aviary.'

'What are you doing?' said Natasha.

'Clive, aviary. Feed time then bed.' Kezia threw a handful of nuts and other treats through the mesh, scattering across the floor of the aviary.

Clive began moving inside Natasha. A pressure grew in her chest and head, then behind her eyes. She turned to the open door of the aviary, but it narrowed in front of her, becoming no wider than her outstretched hand. 'Let us in, Kezia. Let us in.'

Panic now ran through Natasha like acid, and her skin stretched as Clive pushed and pulled inside her. 'Kezia!'

'Clive, aviary,' repeated Kezia. The crows inside squawked in the dark. They hopped from one suspended branch to another, or clung to the wire walls, hissing and rattling, their eyes glinting in the moonlight.

'Stop it, Kezia, now,' said Natasha, gripping the mesh wall with both hands as Clive pulled out of her. She let out a pained cry as the crow emerged, his black presence deforming her skin, his talons clawing at Natasha's mind as his wings folded out, seeking the aviary, and then, with one great beating effort, the crow moved through into the enclosure. He dropped to the ground and pecked at the scattered feed.

Natasha clung to the wire wall, crying out for Clive. She slumped to the ground, saying, 'Kezia, please don't take him away.'

The wind was cold on Natasha's face. She closed her eyes to better feel the fine rain on her cheeks. She inhaled, the air sweet and fresh on the slopes of Arthur's Seat, high above the city. She opened her eyes and looked across Edinburgh. It sat there, stuck forever beneath the grey sky.

Natasha took her phone from her jacket pocket and Andrew's card from the pocket in her jeans. She sat on the grass and took a deep breath. She dialled the number and pressed call.

'Hello,' said Andrew at the end of the line, sounding as if he couldn't quite hear above the background noise of drilling and construction.

Natasha cleared her throat. 'Andrew. Hi, it's Natasha. From the loop.'

'Natasha, hi... Hang on a second.'

More drilling, people talking, shouting. Andrew's voice, saying something to someone. Natasha regretted making the call, and for a moment considered hanging up. Then the noise stopped.

'Natasha. Sorry about that. It's great to hear from you. How are you doing?'

'I'm fine, thanks. I just wanted to say sorry for the other night. I was a bit out of it, I think.'

'Not a problem. Did you get home alright?'

'Yes, I took a taxi.'

'Good,' said Andrew. 'How's work?'

Natasha watched a gull as it hovered above the slopes of the hill. 'I'm taking a few days off. I'm sat on Arthur's Seat right now, watching a seagull. It's bloody freezing.'

Andrew laughed. 'You and your birds.'

Another gull joined the first and together they rode the unseen currents. Natasha felt the same strange pang of loss that she'd tried to describe to Kezia the previous day. A sense of loss tempered by a steely, stubborn pride. Something avian, animal. Something new. 'I was wondering if you'd like to do something,' she said. 'I mean, go out or something. Sorry, I'm not good at this.'

'That would be great. I mean, yes.'

They laughed.

'Good,' said Natasha. 'I'll call you later. I've got to get off this hill.'

Andrew laughed again. 'Okay. Talk later.'

Natasha hung up. She smiled, pulled her bobble hat down over the tips of her cold ears and called Kezia.

'Hi, Nat. How's the holiday?'

'Cold,' said Natasha. 'How's Clive?'

'Well, I'm fine, thanks for asking. And Clive is hanging out with Aarnav, who's forgotten about criminal charges and is now talking about fame and fortune and uploading himself to the cloud.'

Natasha laughed. 'I'll be back at work soon. I feel good.' The two gulls had gone, away to somewhere on the rising wind, above the city and the quiet hum of humanity.

'Don't rush, but the sooner you're back, the better. We've got a lot of shit to sort out, Nat. Clive is amazing. It's a full-on mind upload. Aarnav's even teaching him to construct the virtual space. We've gone *way* beyond, my friend.'

'I know. But we're good. We'll make this work.'

'Alright, Nat. Speak later.'

'Bye, Kez.'

Natasha slid her phone into her pocket and rubbed her cold hands together. She got to her feet and stood above the city, remembering a promise she'd made to be happy. It would be alright. They would be fine. They would make it work.

Because Clive was a clever bird.

THE AUTHORS

Chase Anderson received his degree in Journalism with a minor in Creative Writing at the Rochester Institute of Technology, where he learned to blend science and technology with the craft of storytelling. He lives in the San Francisco Bay Area and works for Alibris, where he handles marketplace integrations, marketing, and identification of his coworkers' backyard birds.

Die Booth is a queer indie author who likes wild beaches and exploring dark places. When not writing, he DJs at *Last Rites* – the best (and only) goth club in Chester, UK. You can read his prize-winning stories in anthologies from Egaeus Press, Flame Tree Press and many others. His books, including his cursed new novella *Cool S*, are available online. You can find out more about his writing at diebooth.wordpress.com or say hi on Bluesky **diebooth.bsky.social**

Tabitha Carless-Frost is a queer writer based in East London, currently studying for an MA in Creative Writing at Royal Holloway, supervised by Eley Williams and Lavinia Greenlaw. They are interested in the ways queerness, magic, language, trauma, and ecology intersect within literary non-fiction. They are currently working on their first book, an auto-fictional consideration on how language, lineage, and legibility converge in rituals of grave attendance and inherited family trauma. Their writing has been stocked at Treadwell's Books and has appeared in *t'ART magazine*, *Crumble*, *Horizon Magazine*, *Mxogyny* online, and the Museum of Sex Objects.

Matthew R. Davis is a Shirley Jackson Award-nominated, Australian Shadows Award-winning author and musician based in Adelaide, South Australia, with around eighty short stories published across the world. His books include *If Only Tonight We Could Sleep* (Things in the Well, 2020), *Midnight In The Chapel of Love* (JournalStone, 2021), *The Dark Matter of Natasha* (Grey Matter Press, 2022), and *Bites Eyes: 13 Macabre Morsels* (Brain Jar Press, 2023). His life partner is the art photographer Red Wallflower. Find out more at matthewrdavisfiction.wordpress.com.

Tony Dunnell lives in a Peruvian jungle town on the edge of the Amazon rainforest, where the people are happy and the insects are big. His stories have appeared in *Daily Science Fiction, MetaStellar, Sci Phi Journal* and more. You can read more of his writing at tonydunnell.com.

James Dwyer lives in Midleton, Cork. He works as a writer by day and a martial arts instructor by night. He has published short stories in anthologies with Beagle North, Anansi Archive, Temple Dark Books, and Sans. PRESS, and writes science fiction and fantasy novels with Indie Publishers, Paused Books. When not enjoying time with his wife and kids, James loves nothing more than to read, write, and fight. To find out more about any of James's other works, check out **@jamesdwyerwriter** on Instagram or Facebook.

Seán Finnan is a writer and researcher from Longford. He is a PhD candidate in the School of Media in TU Dublin.

Sara Maria Greene is an American writer living outside Philadelphia with her husband and four-year-old daughter. She has been published and won honours for her short fiction from many lovely publications, including *Room* and *NPR*. She is currently seeking representation for a short story collection featuring women exploring the depths of human experience with a mix of dark humour, fairy tales, and pleasant absurdity, titled *This Will Be Yours When I Die*. Lovers of fractured fairy tales and unhinged women should visit her website: SaraMariaGreene.com or follow **@SaraMariaGreene**

Michael Imossan is a Nigerian writer with an award-winning chapbook, *For the Love of Country and Memory* (Poetrycolumnnd, 2022) as well as a gazelle, *A Prelude to Caving* (KSR, 2023).

Jesse Krenzel's short fiction has appeared in *Silver Blade, bosque (the magazine), The Santa Barbara Literary Journal,* and the anthologies *Delirium Corridor* and *The Dead Shall Sleep No More Vol. II.* Two of his short stories have also been performed on Hawk & Cleaver's U.K. podcast *The Other Stories.* He currently lives in the Sierra Foothills of Northern California with his wife, pets, and guitars. Jessekrenzel.com

Chris Kuriata lives in the Niagara Region of Canada. His novel *Sacrifice of the Sisters Lot* will be published by Palimpsest Press in October 2023.

Shelley Lavigne writes queer dark fiction. They live in Ontario where they roam their neighbourhood in search of haunted houses and cool bugs. You can also find them online at shelleylavigne.com.

e rathke writes about books and games at radicaledward.substack.com. A finalist for the 2022 Baen Fantasy Adventure Award, he is the author of *Howl* and several other forthcoming novellas. His short fiction appears in *Mysterior Magazine, luminescent machinations, Shoreline of Infinity,* and elsewhere.

Sidney Stevens has an MA in Journalism from the University of Michigan. Her short stories have appeared in numerous literary journals, including *The Woven Tale Press, Oyster River Pages, Hedge Apple, The Wild Word, Philadelphia Stories, Bright Flash Literary Review, The Centifictionist,* and *The Power of the Pause,* an anthology from Wising Up Press. Her creative non-fiction has been published in *Newsweek, The Dillydoun Review, New Works Review,* and *Nature's Healing Spirit,* an anthology from Sowing Creek Press. In addition, she's published hundreds of non-fiction articles and co-authored four books on natural health. See www.sidney-stevens.com

Johanna Antonia Zomers is a playwright with Stone Fence Theatre and writes a weekly column for a Canadian newspaper. Her first novel, *When the Light Enters,* was published with Pastora de la Vega Press. She is at work on a sequel and a collection of essays. She currently lives on a farm in the Donegal Settlement in Ontario and spends creative winters in Spain and Ireland.

Printed in Great Britain
by Amazon

38733446R00138